The bend in the river
has places where the current
reverses itself.
Maybe it is a place where time could go backward
and forward at the same moment.
Here at the eddy with Clay,
like the old days,
it feels possible.

I speak,
playing our old game—

Tell Me Three Things.

There is only one rule.
You have to tell the truth.

THREE THINGS I KNOW ARE TRUE

a novel

BETTY CULLEY

HARPER TEEN

An Imprint of HarperCollinsPublishers

HarperTeen is an imprint of HarperCollins Publishers.

ISBN 978-0-06-290803-2

Typography by Chris Kwon

22 23 24 25 26 LBC 6 5 4 3 2

❖

First paperback edition, 2021

For those who find the beauty
in a life they didn't choose or expect

THREE THINGS
I KNOW
ARE TRUE

PART ONE

Hands

My brother Jonah's nurses
say I have
good hands.

I don't tell anyone that
my hands are only good
when they want
to be good.

I can feel them changing.
Not thinking whose body
they are connected to—
me, the good girl, Liv.

Not noticing,
when they're inspired,
how they are
getting me in trouble.

Jonah's hands are still now,
even though he's only seventeen.

It's not his choice anymore—
hands under the covers
or on top.

We get to decide—
Mom, the nurses,
and me,
his fifteen-year-old sister.

Is that how it is in families,
one child with bad hands,
one child with good?

Jonah's bad hands found a gun
in Clay's attic.

Waved it in the air,
twirled it around his fingers,
held it to his head.

That's not a toy.
It could be loaded.
You know my dad,
Clay told Jonah.

Clay is a serious boy,
not a daredevil
like Jonah.

He wouldn't climb
the cell phone tower
barefoot,
just because it was there.

Clay knows
he doesn't have superpowers.

Mom's lawyer says it's best
if Clay doesn't come here
anymore.

Even though he lives
right across the street.

Clay

When Clay's door opens,
it happens.
My hands are above my head,
waving,
then they are beckoning.

Clay takes a step forward
like my hands have the power
to move him.

Then an invisible force
pulls him backward,
back into his house.

I think he smiles at me.
Maybe not with his mouth,
but definitely with his eyes.

After he disappears,
my empty hands
hold each other,
doubling their strength.

Jonah

Jonah's nurses love him.
They bathe him, comb his hair,
put him in blue shirts
to match his eyes.

Above and beyond,
my mother says grimly,
when I point it out—
like it's a fault.

I lie next to Jonah
and kiss the palm of his hand.
Smack Smack

His face changes
just a little
when I kiss him.

For the past five months
the living room is Jonah's—
a hospital bed
nurse stuff
Jonah's liquid food.

Mom doesn't like it
when I call Jonah's formula pump on wheels
his Food Truck

When I call his suction machine
Suck-It-Up
When I call the new nurses
Contestants
in the JONAH PAGEANT.

Mom says we're lucky
to get any nursing help
at all,
out here in the little mill town
of Maddigan, Maine.

I think,
can you still
call us a mill town
if the mill is closed?

I greet the new nurse, Vivian.
I like her black curly hair
twisting out of its bun.
I like her dark eyes that pause on me,
and her long eyelashes that blink
closed and open, closed and open.
I see her notice the dishes in the sink,
the stains on the linoleum floor,
the laundry piled on the kitchen table,
but look past them to Jonah.

See her pick up Jonah's hand
and kiss it,
just like I do.

Jonah's face relaxes,
and Vivian gets my vote.

Mom is suing Clay's father
for a million dollars
for the loss of a son.

Jonah is still here, I say to her.

She gives me a hard look.
I know you are not that stupid.

I AM that stupid, I answer,
giving her back my own hard look.

I do know how expensive it is
to be helpless.
How many things don't count
as necessary.
A wheelchair ramp
A wheelchair van
Clothes, air-conditioning, prayer cards.
Everything has to be for my brother now.
Jonah doesn't ask for anything,
but he needs everything.

The Attic

How it happened.

Clay's mom, Gwen, says,

Boys, could you please
bring down the boxes of
Halloween decorations
from the attic.

Then we hear the shot.

It's only afterward
that we know it was
THAT shot—
not Clay's dad's
weekend target shooting
in their backyard.

BOOM
It sounds so close.

It's a Saturday, but
I should have known
this BOOM
was different.

Target shooting is
boom boom boom
boom boom boom
boom boom boom.
This is one BOOM.

Even inside our house,
Mom and I
hear Gwen's screams.

Then we see her
in front of her house,
still screaming.

When Jonah is carried
out of Clay's house
there are so many people
around him,
moving so fast
to get him into the ambulance.

My hands hide themselves
in fists.
Part of me
wants to yell at Jonah,

What stupid thing
have you done now?
I'm not going to cover for you
this time.

Clay walks
out of the house,
then is gone in a police car.
His head is down
and I can't see his face.

Lounge

At the hospital
Mom and I wait
in a room.

Two years ago,
we waited in a room
like this one
after Dad had his heart attack—
me and Mom and Jonah.

The hospital has special rooms
for people to wait
for bad news.
The woman who showed us
to the room
called it a "lounge."

*Would you like something to drink,
while you're waiting in the lounge?*
she asks us.

No,
Mom says,
with not even a thank-you.

What are my choices?
I ask the lounge woman.

Mom hits out at my arm
with a snap of her hand.

Tea, coffee, water, juice, milk,
the woman lists.

I'll take apple juice,
if you have it.

She brings me a tiny can
of apple juice
and pours it into an even tinier
paper cup.
It's warm
and tastes like metal.

Different bad-news people
give us updates.

He's in surgery.
He's holding his own.
They are getting ready to
close up.
The doctor will be out
to talk to you soon.

Each time it's just
one person
in the doorway,
Mom lets out a sigh.

I remember, too,
when we waited to hear
about Dad,
and two people came
together.

That must be a bad-news rule.
One person never brings
the worst news
alone.

The whole time
I'm waiting in the lounge,
I keep expecting
Jonah to knock
at the door—
dressed in jeans
and a T-shirt—
having somehow convinced
his doctors
that they have gotten
the wrong patient—
that it was all
a big mistake.

Town Facts

Dad was born here
in Maddigan,
in a farmhouse
on the edge of town.

It burned to the ground
when I was little.

Now it's just a field
with tall grass.

That's where the house was,
Dad told us,
every time we drove by.

It was the same
with other places in town.
The bakery
used to be a barbershop.
The pizza place
was a shoe store.

The way he talked,
everything was once
something else,
with only Dad to remember
what it was.

Jonah would joke,
Is this going to be on the exam, Dad?

I didn't pay much attention
to Dad's town facts.

Now, if I want to know,
he's not here to ask.

Pedaling

The nurses call it
range of motion.
Vivian takes Jonah's
arms and legs
through the motions
he used to make
on his own.

One motion
for his legs
looks like he's pedaling
a bike.

It was Jonah
who taught me
how to ride my bike.

The bike had
old training wheels,
so bent
they barely touched the ground.

Dad tried first.
He gave the bike a hard push,
and yelled,
You got it, Liv. You got it.
I didn't get it.

I won't let you fall,
Jonah said,
and ran next to me,
cheering,
Pedal, pedal, pedal, pedal.

Every time I swayed,
he was there
to grab the handlebars,
until my feet learned
to do it
on their own.

Vivian slow-motions
Jonah's legs.
Pedal, pedal, pedal, pedal.

Snowstorm

At school
I stop hearing the teachers' voices.
It sounds like buzzing in my ears,
all the words blending together
into one big GRAH
coming out of their mouths.

I stop taking notes.
What's the use in writing
GRAH GRAH GRAH?

Behind my book in geometry class
I make snowflakes.

Fold and fold, fold and fold,
and cut out little triangles.

There are triangles in geometry.
GRAH GRAH GRAH.
Mr. Sommers points to them
on the blackboard.
A girl next to me raises her hand
and answers.
BLIH BLIH BLIH

My paper snowflakes are astonishing.
Open all the folds and LOOK—
by snipping away some of the paper

I created something that is more
than just a piece of paper.

How can there be more when there is less?

Mr. Sommers is standing behind my seat
admiring my snowflakes
or not.

I see him remember Jonah,
the boy in his geometry class
two years ago—
wavy brown hair like mine,
and blue eyes instead of my
muddy ones,
the school's star
pole-vaulter and triple jumper.

My whole life
I'm always two grades
behind Jonah.

I lift up a snowflake.
One for you, Mr. Sommers, I say,
and he takes it
as if he can't
say no to me.

My best friend, Rainie,
says it's illegal
to put things

that are not mail
into a mailbox,
but I stuff the snowflakes
in Clay's mailbox
at the end of his driveway.
Our Number 23 mailbox
faces his 24.

I was ten
and Jonah was twelve
when Clay moved in
across the street.

Jonah saw
a boy his age,
skateboarded
down our driveway
across the road
and up Clay's driveway
to introduce himself.
Clay's hair was
lighter than brown
darker than blond
and he was just a little bit taller
than Jonah.

It was fall
and Jonah
picked a pear off a tree
on Clay's front lawn
and handed it to him.

Jonah and Clay
started talking,
and I didn't think Clay
noticed me
standing in front of our house,
but suddenly
he held up the hand
that had the pear,
and waved it at me.

That's the way it was
with Clay and me—
he was Jonah's friend,
but he never acted like
I wasn't there.

I hope it is Clay and not his parents
who find the storm.

Gwen

People in town write letters to the paper.
"A man has a right to have guns in his house."

Even Gwen has a gun—
a small one she keeps in her purse.

No talking back to your mama now,
Jonah said to Clay,
after Gwen told the boys
she carried a handgun
to protect herself,
she's packing heat.

What color is it?
I asked Clay when I heard Jonah
tease him.
It's just a gun, he said,
they don't come in colors.

I didn't ask him what she was afraid of.
Sometimes my hands
make themselves into guns,
but they are careful
not to point at anything.

Straws

I take photos of Jonah
with my phone.
The back of his neck,
his toes,
his fingers curled in on themselves.
Never the whole Jonah.

Mom says NO
to posting them
on his Instagram,
even though this is
his status now.
Many parts that add up
to his new whole.

Jonah has a special machine
to lift him out of bed.
I call it his Trapeze.

Ready to be an acrobat, Jonah?
Your Trapeze is here.

I think his eyes shine brighter
when he is suspended
over the bed.

Does he imagine
his body has grown wings?

I reach out
on the cafeteria line.
Instead of food
I fill my tray with straws.

I twist the plastic straws
into eight-legged spiders—
lots of them.

My friends laugh at the spiders.
Dangle them in each other's faces.
Piper, Justine, Rainie talking
Plah Ha Plah Ha Plah

I can hear the sounds
but not the words.

I imagine that is how Jonah
hears the world now.

Snowflake

That boy across the street
sure has a fascination
with this house,
Vivian says.
He stood there last night
with the snow falling on his head,
just staring.
He's always alone,
never see any friends.

His name is Clay is all I say,
as if that explains everything.
Clay, I say again,
imagining the snow falling
on both our heads.

At first I think I am dreaming—
but there it is—
a paper snowflake
in an upstairs window—
Clay's room.

My hands touch my face
like they've never felt tears before.

Mom's Lawyer

Mom's lawyer says
if there's a trial
he will need a video of Jonah,
if Jonah can't be there.
He looks uncomfortable
in our kitchen.
No place on the messy table
for his brown leather briefcase.

My hands don't move
to make room.

HERE, I scroll through my phone.
I HAVE VIDEOS.
I show him the one
I took
of Jonah in bed—
his face half hidden
under the sheet,
making a humming noise
in his sleep.

He hands me back the phone
I don't think we can use this, Liv.
We'll need to present what is called
a day in the life of Jonah,
done by a professional videographer.

He raises his voice a little
when he says the word
professional.

Later Mom makes excuses,
He does care.
See, he remembered your name.

I don't answer
but I clap slowly—
one two three—
having the last word.

The reminder is always there—
a dent
on the right side
of Jonah's forehead.
The spot you'd press
when you felt a headache
coming on.
The bullet tore away bone
the way dynamite blasts rock—
leaving a soft
crater.

Mom turns away
when the nurses
put cream on
Jonah's boo-boo.

Tray Art

Next time, I fill my cafeteria tray
with mayonnaise, ketchup, mustard.
My hands invent Tray Art.
Squeezing the ketchup packets
in a big circle.
Making wavy lines with the mayonnaise.
Adding dabs
of mustard.

Kids from other tables
stop by
to watch.
Other kids toss over
more art supplies.

I'm opening a new pack
of mustard
when the lunch monitor
comes behind me
and picks up the tray.

Follow me, please, Liv,
she says.

Inside the principal's office
the school counselor
has a lot
of questions.

What do we have here, Liv?
What were you thinking?
Wasting all this food?
Encouraging other students
to do the same?
You realize someone has to
clean this tray?
How respectful is that
of the cafeteria staff?

The lunch monitor
carried the tray carefully—
there's only a few flecks
of ketchup
dotting the mayo.
I smooth them out
with my thumb.

I don't say it's
a red sun
streaked with yellow,
melting a river of ice.
No one asks
whose heart needs melting.

My punishment—
suspension of cafeteria privileges
(I can eat lunch
at an extra desk
in the main office)

and four afternoons
helping at the soup kitchen in town.

Maybe that will teach you
the value of food,
he says.

Maybe, I say,
I know the value of food,
just not of condiments.

That gives me
four more afternoons.

Trap

Mom doesn't call Jonah
by his name anymore.
Jonah is
He
Your brother.

FYI, I tell her,
your son's name is Jonah.

Watch your mouth,
Mom warns me.

She turns off Suck-It-Up,
and starts up Food Truck,
paying more attention
to Jonah's machines
than to Jonah.

Sometimes the moans don't stop.
Ah-rah Ah-rah Ah-rah
Something hurts
but Jonah can't say what.
Ah-rah Ah-rah Ah-rah
Vivian tries
everything.
It sounds
like an animal
caught in a trap.

Not that I've heard one,
but I can imagine.

That's when she gets me
and my good hands.
I smooth Jonah's hair,
pat his cheek,
sing.
Help him find a way
out of the trap.

Once,
Jonah's nurse Johnny
called Mom at Tractor Barn
where she works
when Jonah would not stop.
A-GAH A-GAH A-GAH
Mom came home
and stood by Jonah's bed,
watching.

The sounds Mom made
were worse than Jonah's.
So now the nurses
call me.

Bumper Stickers

When Clay's father's car
is parked in their driveway,
I can read his bumper stickers
from our kitchen window.

"Guns don't kill people.
People kill people."

"If you outlaw guns,
only outlaws will have guns."

There's one more bumper sticker
I try not to look at.

"Gun control means using
both hands."

Clay's father's work van
doesn't have bumper stickers,
just a sign on each side
with a cartoon drawing
of a big bug running away
and the words
Bugz Away
Pest Management.

36

Clay dropped out of school.
I don't blame him.
Who would want to be there
mind reading
what everyone is thinking?

What happened in the attic, Clay?
Did you dare Jonah
to pull the trigger, Clay?
I thought you two were
best friends.
Did you know the gun
was loaded?
Why were you guys
up in the attic, anyway?
How much blood
was there?
Did Jonah have any
last words?

I'll never work for my Dad,
Clay used to say.

Work must be better
than school—
because he does now.

What kinds of bugs
does he manage?
I once asked Clay.

All kinds—whatever people
don't want.

How does he "manage" them?
I made air quotes.

You're not serious, are you, Liv?
Clay said softly then.
He had more patience
for me
than Mom.

I have a theory about
friendship.
One friend is always nicer.
Jonah made everyone laugh.
He could talk to anyone
about anything,
but Clay was nicer.

Soup Kitchen

Elinor is the boss
of the soup kitchen.
Her hair is all white,
even though she doesn't look
much older than Mom,
and she wears a white apron
that is longer
than her dress.

She gives me an apron
that matches hers.

I think Elinor's been warned
about me,
because right away
she keeps me busy:
rolling silverware into paper napkins,
loading the dishwasher,
serving shepherd's pie
with a long-handled spoon.
I like that
Elinor doesn't ask questions,
doesn't try to be my friend.
The rhythm of the work
is like a dance:
roll, roll, in and out,
ladle, ladle, ladle.

If my hands are tired enough
maybe they will sleep.

At the end of the shift,
I cut food.
I guess my hands passed some test
to be trusted with a knife.
First potatoes, then carrots,
then onions.
Elinor stares at the cutting board
she gave me.

The pieces don't all have to be
the same size. This is not a
factory,
Elinor comments.

Okay, I can do that,
I answer.

Snowman

Jonah's nurse Johnny
has a big laugh,
strong arms,
and a shaved head.
He's from the South
and this is his first winter
in Maine.
When he says the snow
is sticking in the trees,
it gives me an idea.

I remember that
sticking snow
is snowball snow.
I build a snowman
next to the holly
in the side yard.
It's been a long time
since we rolled snowballs—
Jonah and I—
but it's not rocket science.
Big one for the bottom
Medium one for the middle
Smallest one on top.

From behind the holly,
I study Number 24.

This past Thanksgiving
and Christmas,
there weren't any decorations
on the house
or the lawn.
No cardboard turkeys
or pumpkins.
No big red bow
on the mailbox.
And no Clay knocking
at our door
with a homemade apple pie
from Gwen.

I speak my words
into the swirling snow
but they don't reach
across the street.

It's me. Liv.
I'm still here, Clay.

I decorate my snowman
with Jonah's sunglasses
for the glare—
and put one of Jonah's Red Sox hats
on top,
brim facing backward—
his signature look.

The next morning
I laugh
when I see that the snowman
has earbuds.
Why does laughing
feel so much like crying now?

Jonah

Sometimes the cries are different—
Wah-AH Wah-AH Wah-AH
It's dark out, and
I stand there in my Hello Kitty pajamas.
Johnny, out of nurse tricks,
shakes his head and
raises his hands in the air.

This time it feels like Jonah
is calling to me
from a distance,
trying to get back home,
but the ground cracks open
before him
each time he takes a step.

Sometimes,
there is nothing anyone can do.

Line

There's an invisible line
in the middle of the road
between my house and Clay's.
When I go out to wait
for the school bus,
Clay's mom
comes to the middle of that line.

Liv, please leave Clay be.
I've seen how he looks
across the street.
Don't make things worse
than they already are.

Really, Gwen, I take a step forward,
do you think things could be WORSE
for us?

She looks down at the pavement.
I see her mouth open
like she wants to
say something—
but doesn't.

Hunter

Hunter from school is there
at the soup kitchen.
He's homeschooled,
but he goes to school
for what he wants—
like orchestra and
civil rights team
and French.
I can't see Mom
letting me have a deal
like that.

Hunter knows the drill.
He takes an apron
off a hook
and puts it on.
He ties it in front.
The white apron
makes his red hair
seem even redder.

What did they get you for?
I ask him.

What do you mean?
he says.

Why you're here?
Throw your sandwich on the floor?
Spit out your lunch?
Play with your food?

I've been volunteering
this past year—
when it fits into my music schedule,
he says.

Yeah, I know,
you got that violin thing.

Hunter gets his own knife
and cutting board.
I push the bag of onions
toward him.
It's time for someone else
to cry.

Birthdays

When is Jonah's birthday?
Vivian wants to know.
We could have a little party.
Jonah can't blow out candles
but does he have a wish
somewhere deep inside?
If Jonah doesn't use his wish
can I have it?

Big planning starts for Jonah's
eighteenth birthday
next month.
The nurses love a party.
Vivian tapes a food sign-up sheet
on the fridge.
So far, there's brownies,
broccoli quiche, and fruit punch.
No worries about what
to serve Jonah.
All his food
goes in his tube.

My birthday is the same week—
Sweet Sixteen.
This year
will be the first
without a present
from Jonah.

He used to hint
that my sixteenth
would be extra special,
but now
I'll never know
what he meant.

Dead End

Believe it or not
at the end of our street
it says DEAD END.
When we moved in,
that was good news.
Mom said
DEAD END meant safety
riding bicycles
skateboards
trick-or-treating.

Besides DEAD END,
it was extra cheap—
the paper mill
right behind us
belching a stench
we got used to.

Does it always smell like this?
people from away would ask.
No, we'd joke,
it usually smells worse.

The smell was sulfur
from the pulping process,
making supercalendered paper
for the *New York Times*
Sunday supplement.

Now the mill is closed,
and it's hard to get a job.
Unless you're lucky enough
that your dad owns
Bugz Away Pest Management.

The brick mill
with its tall smokestacks
is on the river
that was the highway
for the logs,
the place to dump
the sludge,
the hydropower
for the paper machines
my father used to fix.
I can walk to the river
from the house.
The river is the same
as it always was,
wide, shining, moving
in spring, summer, and fall,
frozen in winter.

I ask Mom
why we don't sell
Number 23
and move off DEAD END.

She says that since the mill closed,
no one is looking to buy a house
in Maddigan.

I don't know if that's the real reason
or if it's a game of chicken.

We don't move
and neither does Clay's family.

It's like moving
would be saying
we take the blame.

Coffee

Hunter is back.

I guess it fit
into your music schedule,
I say.

I'm not doing this for college,
if that's what you think,
he says.
Sometimes I'd rather be here
than home.
It's quieter here,
and I can think better.

Got it,
I answer,
and I do.

I haven't yet seen
soup in the soup kitchen.
Tuna noodle casserole,
mac and cheese,
beef stew
are all popular.
And coffee.
The coffee urn
is like a statue in a church,

not that I go to church.
People gather around it
and worship.
I never drank coffee before,
but I try my first cup
and I'm hooked.

The Eddy

Sometimes a word gets through
to me in school.
Like watching a show in Swedish
and an actress says *okay*.
It was like that in world history today.

Demilitarized zone.

It makes me think of the eddy—
the bend in the river
where Jonah, Clay, Rainie, Piper,
Justine, and I used to meet
on Saturday nights.

Mom always said,
*Don't go down to the river
in the dark.*
It's not dark, we'd say.
It's half dark.
It was always half dark,
once our eyes adjusted.

When it's half dark
on Saturday,
I go down to the river,
and it's all still there.

The cement boat ramp,
the aluminum dock,
the roiled river,
full with the winter's
ice melt,
running fast and muddy
the way it does every March.

"Demilitarized zone."

How could I have forgotten?

It's cold at the ramp,
the wind rough off the river.
There's still patches of snow
along the banks.

Clay is there.
Even in the half dark,
he looks skinnier,
his hair longer
like he's trying to hide himself.
I can't guess how I look
to him.

I came down here
every Saturday
the last five months,
Clay tells me,

*I wanted to know
how you were doing.*

Sorry, I say, *I was busy.*

Clay looks out at the river.

*I texted you about
a thousand times,*
I say.

*I got rid of my phone
five months ago,*
he says.

The bend in the river
has places where the current
reverses itself.
Maybe it is a place where time could go backward
and forward at the same moment.
Here at the eddy with Clay,
like the old days,
it feels possible.

I speak,
playing our old game—

Tell Me Three Things.

There is only one rule.
You have to tell the truth.

I think about Clay's father's
Bugz Away van.

Tell me three things
about bedbugs,
I say.

Clay holds up
one finger.
Bedbugs do not fly.
Second finger.
They can survive for a year
without a blood meal.
Third finger.
Adult bedbugs
are about the size
of an apple seed.

I forgot how good Clay is
in science—
in middle school,
he did an experiment
measuring pollution
in the river
downstream from the paper mill.

My father
was alive then,
and he still had his job
at the mill.
Millwright

on the night shift,
keeping the big machines running.
When Clay asked,
my father told him all about
the chemicals
they used.

Methanol
Ammonia
Hydrogen sulfide
Hydrochloric acid

The hydrogen sulfide
gave our town
its smell.

When the smell
went away,
so did the jobs.

The paper mill
sponsored the school science fair.
You can guess that
Clay didn't win a prize.

How is your mother?
Clay asks me.
(That's what I mean
about Clay being nicer.)

Scary, I say,
and he looks away.
I don't ask about Gwen.

My hand reaches out to his
and holds it
for the first time,
like I hold Jonah's now.

This is my science experiment.
Do all boys' hands feel the same?
His is cold
yet a little sweaty
in a nice way.
It squeezes back.
That never happens
with Jonah.

Since Jonah came home
from the hospital,
I've gotten to know every inch
of a boy's body.
I thought there were
no mysteries.
But holding Clay's hand
is like hearing
a foreign language—
I can only guess
what is being said.

Hippies

I peel carrots away from me.
Hunter peels them toward himself.
It's not supposed to be
a contest,
but I know I'm right.
Peeling away goes faster.

Why are you here?
Hunter asks.

Tray art.

I don't elaborate.
It's good to leave something
to the imagination.

Maybe we can get together
sometime,
Hunter says,
you could come to my house,
if you don't mind a crowd
of kids.

How many is a crowd?
I ask.

Oldest of six.
First they created the

babysitter,
Hunter taps his chest,
then the rest of the babies.

Like a blended family,
his kids, her kids,
their kids together?
I ask him.

No, my mom
really loves babies.
My parents are kinda
back-to-the-land
hippies.

My father used to say
there were two kinds of
hippies
in Maine.
The trust-fund hippies
and the don't-know-what-they're-getting-into
hippies,
I say.

I guess then we're the
don't-know-what-we're-getting-into ones.

It occurs to me
that even repeating something
not so nice
is not nice.

Sorry, that's just something
my father used to say.
He was born in Maine.

So were my parents,
Hunter says.

Memory Metal

Every day in chemistry class,
I open my textbook
to the same page.
It lists the names and numbers
and nicknames
of the elements
that make up everything
in the world.

Antimony, 51, Sb
Tantalum, 73, Ta
Californium, 98, Cf

They don't make any more sense
than the rest of the sounds
I hear in class.

Ms. Roy fits red and green balls
on the ends of plastic sticks.
They're called molecular models
but to me
they look like dog chew toys.

She holds one up,
her mouth moves,
and these sentences break through:

A memory metal is an alloy
that remembers its original shape.
If the material has been de-formed
it will regain its original shape
when it is reheated or left alone.

Does Jonah remember
his original form?
We can't ever
leave him alone.

Team Meeting

Team Meeting for Jonah.
All his nurses
Me
Dr. Kate
making a house call.

Mom can't take the time
off work
again.

We crowd in the messy kitchen.
I don't have an urn,
but I make coffee
in the coffeemaker,
set out sugar and cream.

I guess I learned something
at the soup kitchen.
Coffee makes a bad situation
better.

Team Meeting is:
discuss what's working,
what isn't.
What the sounds Jonah makes
mean.
Nurse Johnny gives me a
shout-out.

Liv understands Jonah
better than anyone else.

Dr. Kate speaks up,
You'd make an excellent nurse,
Liv, think about it.

Thanks, Dr. Kate,
but I'd rather be a doctor.

Oh, really?
Dr. Kate tries not to look surprised.

Yeah,
I've seen how hard
the nurses work.

Vivian covers her mouth
behind Dr. Kate's back,
but I can still hear the snort.

Fiddle Music

Hunter and I are both serving.
Beef stew
Yeast rolls
Sliced carrots
Peach cobbler

It's not like at school.
In the soup kitchen,
I can hear the words people in line say.
Mostly the talk is about food.

"I was hoping it would be stew."
"No peach cobbler for me,
I'm watching my sugar."
"My mother made the best yeast rolls."

I ask Hunter something.

*Can you play fiddle music
on that violin of yours?*

*What do you mean—
fiddle music?*

Hunter makes a face
like I asked him if he
could shovel snow
with his violin.

Ya know . . .

And I take a clean ladle
from the drawer,
put it on my shoulder
like a fiddle,
tap my foot, and sing.

Old Joe Clark, he had a house
Fifteen stories high
And every story in that house
Was filled with chicken pie.

There is applause, and smiles.
The food line stops moving
but Elinor doesn't look mad.

I smile back
and take a little bow.
This is the silliest I've been
in five months.

That back-to-the-land
baby-loving mother of his
taught Hunter some manners.
He doesn't laugh
at my bad singing.

I suppose if I had the
sheet music, I could.
Why?

My brother Jonah
always liked to listen
to the fiddlers
at the fair.

See, I learned something else
at the soup kitchen.
Music
makes a bad situation
better.

Fleas

I don't lie.
I tell Mom,
I'm going down to the river.
She makes a
faraway face
when I say *river.*

I know all about
how Dad proposed to Mom
in the middle
of the swinging footbridge
over the Kennebec,
before the last big flood
washed it away,
and how they used to
go out in an old rowboat
to pick wild blueberries
along the banks of the river.

Clay is there
in the half dark
at the end of the dock.
It's not windy this time,
and the river is calm.
The Kennebec is very deep,
my dad told us,
eighty feet in the middle.

Clay has a funny smell
like the weed-killer aisle
at Agway.

Something smells weird.
Does your dad have you
spray the poison?

No, it's the truck.
Do you want me to
jump in the river
and wash it off?

We both know
it's about forty degrees
in the water.

Since the Three Things game rule is
you have to be truthful,
I could say,

Tell me three things
about your father
or
Tell me three things
you wish you could undo

but I don't.

I say to Clay,
Tell me three things
about fleas

First Finger.
Fleas are flightless.
Second Finger.
Fleas don't have wings.
Third Finger.
Fleas can jump.

I don't point out that First Finger
and Second Finger
say the same thing.
I'm practicing to be as nice
as Clay.

Clay doesn't ask me
three things
but he reaches out for my hand
and holds my three fingers
with his three fingers.

He doesn't ask
Three things about Jonah.

I'm not sure if I'm glad
or not.

Cold

When Jonah gets a cold
he is restless.
His nose runs
but he can't wipe it,
doesn't know to cough
up the gunk.
He doesn't even have the strength
for loud cries.
Cu-rah cu-rah cu-rah

He can't have
tea and honey.
He'd choke
on a cough drop.

I get into bed with him
in my sweatpants
and unicorn T-shirt.

Liv, I can look after Jonah,
Johnny says.
*You need your sleep
for school tomorrow.*

That's okay,
I say,
*I don't need to be awake
in school.*

I scrunch up between Jonah
and the metal bedrail.
I hear Jonah's chest noises,
feel the warmth of his fever
through his pajamas.
Johnny spreads Jonah's blanket
to cover both of us.
Jonah is less restless
when I'm there.
It's better to be miserable
together.

After Jonah's cold,
his Suck-It-Up machine
gets a playmate—
Zombie Vest.
Zombie Vest jiggles Jonah's
lungs twenty minutes
twice a day,
and Suck-It-Up
gets rid of the gunk.

Dr. Kate tells Mom
Jonah can go to a nursing home
if it is
too much.
He would get
good care.
It would be
round the clock.
No one would

judge her.
Dr. Kate would
fully support her decision.
We could visit
24/7.
Jonah would be in
good hands.

Dr. Kate waits for Mom
to say something.
When Mom doesn't answer,
she adds,

And you could personalize
Jonah's room.

Personalize?
Mom repeats.
You mean like a banner with his name?

Mom says *banner*
like it's a curse word.

Dr. Kate is starting to look sorry
she brought this up.

Not necessarily a banner,
though of course
it could be a banner.
Things like posters,

or sports trophies,
or family photos.

Posters?
Mom gives Dr. Kate
her blank look,
the one that means
"Why are you telling me this?
How about not."
And I know right then,
there is no way
Jonah is going
anywhere.

Ears

The school counselor
wants to *have a chat.*

He does most of the chatting.
*Your teachers say you are not
participating in class
or handing in assignments.*

I lean over his desk
and tap my ears.
*I can't always hear
what's going on.*

He looks relieved.
*Well, I can see that could
be a problem.
I'll make an appointment
for you
with the school audiologist.
In the meantime
I can arrange that you get to sit
up front.*

I raise my hand.
*Oh no, please,
I don't want anyone*

feeling sorrier for me
than they already are.

He gives me a kind
counselor smile.

Got it, Liv.

Elinor

At the soup kitchen
people say
Hi there, singer girl
and talk to me for the first time.
Hunter isn't there.
Elinor and I work in the
walk-in cooler,
checking expiration dates.
Donated food
goes bad, too.

*Only one more afternoon
with us,* Elinor comments.

I'm guessing she's thinking
I'm gonna say
how much l love volunteering
how much I've learned
how I want to keep giving back,
finding meaning here.

*I'd like to come visit
your mother,*
Elinor says.

*I don't know about that.
Mom's kinda busy*

working at Tractor Barn.
Trying to clean the house
on the weekends.

That last part
about the cleaning
isn't exactly true.

Elinor gives me a
mind-reader look,

Your mom and I used to hang out
with the same crowd in high school.
My brother worked with your father
in the mill.
My aunt lives one block over from
where you live.
Maybe some Sunday
your mother has off?

Right, this is a small town.
You don't need to give anyone
your résumé.
They already know everything
they need to know.

That's up to you.
Try giving her a call
is the nicest warning I can think of.

Sounds

The school audiologist
is friendly,
at first.
I like the sounds the machine makes
in my ears.
They remind me of the sounds I hear
in class—
Bip Barp Eet Dud Deep

When we're done
she says she didn't find
any problem
with my hearing.
I scored well
on high-pitched sounds, too.

*Oh, like what a dog hears
or a bat?*
I ask her.
*I forget which animal hears those sounds
or makes them.*

No, she says,
this test is for
PEOPLE.

I confess,
It's more the words
that are the problem,
not the sounds.

I see, she says,
but does she?

River

Next time we meet
at the river,
Clay's hair is wet
and he smells like soap,
but there is still a chemical smell
in the air.
He looks even skinnier.

Are the chemicals slowly
exterminating him
like a bedbug or a flea
or a carpenter ant?
Would the river
wash him clean?
Would it wash
both of us
clean?

I don't have the heart
to play Three Things.
I lie back on the dock
next to Clay.
The snow is gone
from the banks now,
and today for the first time
I heard the loud honking
of Canada geese,
returning north for spring.

If it wasn't half dark
we could see the sky.
So much sky
over the river.

If we fell asleep right here,
I say,
when we woke up
the first thing we'd see
is the sky.

That's true,
Clay says.

He's nice enough
not to point out that
even though it's spring,
we'd freeze
if we tried to sleep outside
this time of year.

Gwen

One morning
Gwen is waiting for me
on the line again
in her bathrobe.

I know about the river,
she says.

What about the river?
The river belongs to
everyone.

Does Clay talk to you there
at the river?
He won't talk to me.
He won't listen
about going back to school.
Can you talk to him?
Please.

It's the *please*
that gets to me,
and the bathrobe
and the fact
that she won't
cross the invisible line.

Talk about what?

Talk about anything.
We don't know
what he's thinking
anymore.
What he wants.

Gwen reaches a hand out
to me.
I tell my hand NO
but it grasps Gwen's
across the line.

I don't know what I have
promised Gwen
or how I will keep
that promise.

Friends

It's decided
my time-out
from the cafeteria
is over.
The office secretary says
she'll miss my company
at lunch.

Rainie, Piper, and Justine
make room for me at the table.
This is what's in my school salad—
two large pieces of lettuce,
brown and curling in on the edges,
four skinny slices of carrot,
one long slice of celery,
two cherry tomato halves.

I think about making a beach bungalow
with my salad.
I could stand four carrots upright
and cover them with the largest
piece of lettuce
for the roof.
For the palm tree—
little cuts in the top of the celery
to make fronds.

Instead I eat a carrot
and the palm tree.

Rainie leans her head against mine.
When we were little
and people said our hair
was the same shade of brown,
we'd say it's 'cause
we're best friends.

We missed you, Liv.
That was so unfair,
Rainie says.

Piper puts the two halves
of the cherry tomatoes
together
and gives them to me.

Justine asks,
So, is Jonah getting better?

It is not my friends' fault
what they say
what they don't say.

I remember the quote
on the blackboard
in English class.

How can you expect a man
who's warm to understand
a man who's cold?

From *One Day in the Life of Ivan Denisovich*
by Aleksandr Solzhenitsyn

Mrs. Osgood asked us,
What do you think that means?

Gavin raised his hand.
It's wicked cold in Russia?

We laughed at that.
I think I could answer
Mrs. Osgood's question
now.

My father had a lecture
Jonah called
Dad's everybody-has-something sermon.
Dad believed we
couldn't judge anyone
'cause we could never really know
what it was like
to walk in someone else's shoes.

Justine doesn't see
how beautiful she is,
how everyone wants
to be her

except her.
She thinks her legs
are too long,
her chest too big,
her hair too thin,
her eyes
too far apart.

Justine's mother died
of an overdose
when she was a baby.
She says she sees her mother
in her dreams,
and is sorry when she
wakes up.

Rainie
can't stop herself
from shoplifting,
even though her father
is a police officer
and she hears his stories.

Her mother has no clue.
I know that Rainie's hands
are in charge
and I
can't judge.

I picture
a small hungry animal
burrowing inside Rainie,
and her hands
finding things to give it,
to make it
less hungry.

Piper worries she'll die
from the superbug
and is afraid of germs
I can't even pronounce.
She is sure
flesh-eating bacteria
are everywhere.
She was born in India
and her mother, Millie,
adopted her
when she was two.
Millie wants to
take her back there
for a visit this summer,
but once Piper heard
the shots she'd need—
against diseases like typhoid
and rabies and yellow fever—
she wouldn't go.

Everybody-has-something.
I have Jonah.

Soup Kitchen

Hunter is back
and his fiddle
is on a chair next to him.

*I got a book
of fiddle music.
I've been practicing
the "Erie Canal" song.
Elinor says we should play
after lunch.*

Hunter looks out at the crowd of people
with the fiddle in his hands,

*I've got a mule and her name is Sal—
Fifteen miles on the Erie Canal.
She's a good old worker and a good old pal—
Fifteen miles on the Erie Canal.*

*We've hauled some barges in our day
Filled with lumber, coal, and hay,
And we know every inch of the way
From Albany to Buffalo.*

His right foot keeps time
like the music
is inside tapping to come out.

Low bridge, everybody down,
Low bridge for we're coming to a town.
And you'll always know your neighbor
And you'll always know your pal
If you've ever navigated on the Erie Canal.

There's laughing and clapping
and waving as people leave.
I turn the urn spigot for a few last drips
of coffee
scoop sugar into it
and raise my cup to Hunter.

That was great.
Jonah's nurses are planning
a birthday party for him.
Would you come and play?

Sure, just let me know when.

He zips his fiddle
into its case.

Of course
in our small town
there's no need to explain
Jonah or *nurses*
to Hunter.

This is your last afternoon,
Elinor says,
as if I hadn't been counting
them off.
Don't be a stranger.

Termites

The days are getting longer
and the half dark comes slower
down by the river.
Are your eyes green or blue or brown
or yellow?
I ask Clay.
Every time I look
I see a different color.
It's like a kaleidoscope.

Mayflies and yellow-eyed crickets
have yellow eyes,
not people.
he says

It's just like Clay
to be studying about bugz
when he is not "managing" them.

Clay points to the half-light sky and then the river.
You're probably just seeing reflections
of colors
in my eyes.

What about my eyes?
I ask Clay

Dark brown with little orange streaks.

You didn't even look at them,
I point out.

You think
after all these years
I don't know
the color of your eyes, Liv?

I turn my face
so Clay can't see
what I'm feeling.

Tell me three things
about termites,
I say.

Clay groans.
Really, Liv?

I poke him in the chest
with my finger.
Play the game.

First Finger.
Only the worker termites
can digest wood.
Second Finger.
They are responsible for
building the mud tubes and nests
for the whole colony.
Third Finger.

Worker termites are blind
and work twenty-four hours a day
for their entire two-year life.

I'm sorry I asked
about termites.
Clay sounds so sad
about the worker termites' life,
I don't know what to say.
That's the problem with the
Three Things game.
You have to tell the truth
and sometimes the truth hurts.

I think about my promise to Gwen.
I did talk to Clay.
We talked about eyes
and termites.
That will have to be enough
for now.

Mom

Mom watches me make
my morning coffee.
She stands at the counter
with one finger
in her mouth.
She's pressing her finger
on a tooth
and I see her flinch
like she just got
an electric shock.
Then she speaks to me.

I hear you're working yourself up
to repeat your sophomore year.
Did you change your mind
about college?
What do you think you'll do
with a tenth-grade education?

I dump an extra spoonful of sugar
in my coffee
and turn around to look at my mother.
Her work shoes are scuffed,
her face is puffy.
It's been a long time
since she's had her hair trimmed.
Even so,

I raise my hands in the air
my palms facing upward,
and shrug my shoulders,
Work at Tractor Barn?

Jonah

Ga-Ga-Ga-Rah Ga-Ga-Ga-Rah
Zombie Vest makes Jonah's sounds
vibrate.
Ga-Ga-Ga-Urgh
Suck-It-Up makes Jonah gag.
Ook Ook Ook
Food Truck
delivers too much supper
and Jonah cries in pain.

Sometimes the machines
are Jonah's friends.
Sometimes they betray him.

When the machines are bad
I put them in the corner
of the room.
I tell Jonah,
Don't worry about Food Truck.
I pressed the Pause button.
And I warned Suck-It-Up
he's next.

There's a calendar
in my head
and all the months
say "Jonah."

Instead of
Monday, Tuesday, Wednesday,
the days are
Good Day, Bad Day.
If there are more Good Days
than Bad Days,
then it's a Good Month.

The Deal

Gwen is very impatient.
She is back on the line
again.
Same faded bathrobe,
accessorized with
worn slippers.

Did you talk to Clay?

I did.

Gwen ties another knot
in the bathrobe belt.

And?

*We talked about eyes
and termites.
It was only one time.*

Muh Muh Muh

Gwen sounds like Jonah,
making sounds but not
words.

I have seen his struggle
so the new nicer me
just waits.

Gwen can't look at my face.

My guh guh . . .
My gun is gone.

I realize she can't speak
the word *gun*
to me
any louder
than a whisper.

You think Clay has it?

I don't know,
Gwen says.

Why don't you ask him?

Gwen lets her arms
hang down by her sides.
We both know she can't
ask him.

Okay,
I say,

okay, I find your
gun
and you move
off this street.

Gwen nods YES
to the deal.

Logs

My dad's father
was a log driver
on the Kennebec River,
this same river
that passes behind our house.
My grandfather rode the logs
down the river
to the mill.
All he had was
spiked shoes
and a pike pole
to push the logs apart
when they jammed together.

As you can guess,
it was dangerous work,
riding a log down
the river.
He watched a friend
slip
between two logs
and drown.

All those years
on the river,
and my grandfather
never knew how to swim.

Even so,
I wish there were still
jobs like that.

Working in the woods
all winter,
standing on water
in the spring.

The log drives
were stopped
because the river
turned brown with tannin
from the bark of the logs,
and the trout died.

Dad said
there are still logs
on the bottom
of the river,
ones that sank
all those years ago.

It's true with logs too.
Some move down the river
where they need to go,
and some sink down,
caught forever
in the mud.

In the Belly of the Whale

I hear Elinor and Mom
in the kitchen.
I stop on the stairs
to listen.

Mom speaks.

I wish I knew
if he is still
in there.
Liv is so
sure.
I don't know how
she does it.

That is more words
than I've heard
Mom say
about Jonah
in five months.

There is silence,
then Elinor speaks.

When Jonah was in the belly of the whale,
who but God could know
what he was thinking,
what he was feeling?

Uh-oh, I think,
Elinor is talking about God
and the Bible.
Even I know there is a Jonah story
in the Bible,
not that Mom named Jonah
for a story.
She just liked the name.

When the Bible people
come to the door,
Mom doesn't answer.
She says it's more polite
that way—
not to open the door
rather than
slam it closed.

I make noise on the stairs
so they know I'm coming.

There is a casserole
on the table.
It looks like tuna noodle,
but it's not in a soup kitchen dish.
I'm happy to see it.
It's been a long time
since Mom and I
ate something hot.

We eat a lot of cereal and milk
and sandwiches.

The kitchen isn't really our kitchen
anymore.
It's where the nurses prepare
Jonah's food,
where they draw up meds,
where they eat their meals.
The nurse schedule is taped
to the refrigerator.
In a kitchen drawer
is a Do Not Resuscitate
form, unsigned.

We share our kitchen
with Jonah's fan club.
It makes things less lonely
and more lonely
at the same time.

Hi, Liv.

I see that Elinor
has an arm around
my mother,
and Mom isn't
shaking it off.

Hi, Elinor,
thanks for the casserole.
It smells great.

Another soup kitchen lesson:
A hot meal
makes you realize
people care.

O

Facts about oxygen:
It is atomic number 8
on the periodic table
of elements.
Its nickname is the letter O.
It was formed
in the heart of stars.

This time Team Meeting
is all about O—
Does Jonah need O?
Would O make Jonah
more comfortable?
This time,
the nurses make sure
Mom is there.

We are not saying Jonah
is worse,
Dr. Kate tells Mom.
We just think it would be
prudent
to have O
on hand.

Mom agrees.
What can she say?

There is enough O
in the air for her,
for me,
for the nurses,
for everyone we know
except Jonah.

I never really thought
about the fact
that invisible O,
something we can't see,
can't hold in our hands,
is keeping us all alive.

River Rats

That's what
people called
the log drivers like my
grandfather.

I look at the water
and wonder if rats can swim.

Before I start to ask Clay
Three things about rats,
he says,

Tell me three things
you know are true.

This is harder than you think.
I've learned
it's hard to really know
another person.
You can't know
the future.
Even the things you see
every day
change.

First Finger.
I know that hands

can speak.
Second Finger.
I know that Jonah
is in there.
Third Finger.
I know I'd rather be here
at the river
with you
than anywhere else.

Then I get up
and leave
before I've asked
what Gwen wants to know
because I've already said too much.

Rainie

The *Kennebec Herald*
is supposed to be
delivered to our house
every day.
Darn it,
Mom says,
someone took the newspaper
again.
Who bothers to go to the trouble
of taking
someone else's paper?

I don't say
I do.
Today there was another
letter to the editor
in the newspaper.

"People blame gun owners for
gun accidents. In my opinion,
that is faulty reasoning. Everyone is
sorry that Jonah Carrier was hurt,
but maybe if his parents had taught
him how to handle a gun and taught
him how to check if a gun was loaded,
in my opinion, this tragedy could have
been avoided."

Today is another day
I stuff the newspaper
in my backpack,
and toss it out
at school.

Rainie is at our door
on Saturday morning.
She wants to go
shop(lift)ing.
Piper and Justine
won't go again
after the last time.

Rainie doesn't come in
farther than the
mudroom.
She's not the only one.

Everyone says
they don't want to
disturb us.

They look away when they
see Jonah's nurses
or hear the sounds
Suck-It-Up makes.

When we say
Come in

they shake their heads
like we can't really mean it.

Rainie wants to go to
the Thriftee Thrift Shop.
We walk down
past the river
into town.

The Thriftee Thrift Shop
(it used to be a pet shop
or a bottle redemption center,
I can't remember which)
smells like wet laundry
that sat in the washing machine
too long.
The front window
is already decorated for spring
with baskets and plastic grass
and a Hula-Hoop—all for sale.

There's a display
of jewelry
in the glass front case.
Rainie asks to see the
tray of earrings,
then the tray of rings,
then the tray of necklaces,
then the tray of rings again.

When I hear Rainie ask
for the tray of rings
again, and say,
I'll take this one,
I know it's coming—
Rainie's own personal
Buy One
Get One Free
deal.

I look for something
for Jonah
for his birthday.
He has enough
blankets,
doesn't really wear out
his clothes,
can't use the baseball mitt
or the chin-up bar.
I see an old harmonica
on a shelf,
and pick it up.

Ugh,
Rainie says,
*who knows what kind of germs
are in that thing.*

She sounds like Piper,
who thinks the superbug
could be hiding anywhere.

No, I'm serious,
you really plan on
putting your mouth on that?

Despite what Rainie says,
I pay the two dollars
plus tax for the harmonica.

Let's stop by the river,
I suggest,
and Rainie says okay.
She's happy now
with her special deal.
She shows me the little ring
with the green stone
that fits on her pinky,
but I can tell she is thinking about the
get-one-free.

We lie facedown
on the dock
and splash our hands
in the water
like when we were little.
The trees on the edge of the bank
seem to hold on to the river
with just their bare roots.

Remember when we'd all
come down here—
you and me, and Jonah and Clay,
and play that game?
The Three Things game?

I remember,
I say.

I'm grateful
to Rainie
that she says his name—
Jonah.
That she never stopped
saying his name.

Rainie takes a necklace
out of her pocket.
It has a silver half-moon pendant.
She dips it in the water
lifts it out
dips it in
lifts it out
then lets it go.

I don't know if
that's a good thing
or not.

Locker

I thought my hands
had learned their lesson
at school,
but there is something
they just have to do.
Open my locker.
Slam it closed.
Open my locker.
Slam it closed.
Open my locker.
Slam it closed.

It *is* my locker.
School is over
and the hallway
is empty.

Open my locker.
Slam it closed.
Open my locker.
Slam it closed.

I can't believe
I never figured
this out before—
how good it feels
to

Open my locker.
Slam it closed.

Something about
metal banging metal,
how it echoes
down the long hallway
of lockers,
makes me happy.

I am slamming
until I am
interrupted.

Mr. Fortunato reaches out
and holds my locker door
before I can slam it again.

Are you having a problem
shutting your locker, Liv?
If you are,
I don't think
this is the best way
to handle it.

It's okay now.
I fixed it.
See?

Mr. Fortunato lets go of the door
and I very, very gently close it
and walk away.

Lip

While we waited
in the bad-news lounge,
surgeons traced the path
of the bullet
through Jonah's brain.
The bullet,
like the gun,
was evidence.

The surgeon said
there would be
"deficits."
They didn't know exactly
what the
"deficits"
would be.
Time would tell.
It was a miracle
he survived.

Speaking of miracles,
me, myself, Liv,
the sometimes good girl,
witnessed
one of Jonah's miracles.
Johnny knows too,
because he was there

the night
Jonah said it.

I was joking with Jonah,
patting one side of his face
and then the other,
soft gentle pats,
my face close to his,
rubbing noses together.

Oh, Jonah,
I asked him,
are you getting enough attention?
Nose rub
Cheek pat
Do you want more attention?
Smoothing his hair back
Getting in his face
What's that face?
You want me to go away?
Leave you alone?
You want a boys' night
just you and Johnny?
No girls allowed?

Jonah took a deep breath.
He looked right back at me,
his mouth worked,
and he said
Li Li Lip

Johnny and I both froze.
If he hadn't heard it.
If I hadn't heard it.
If we hadn't heard it together.

I turned to Johnny,

Don't tell Dr. Kate
Jonah said my name.
She won't believe you,
or she'll try and make him
do it again.
We know we heard it.
He'll say it again
when he wants to.
Don't tell Mom, either.
Let Jonah be the one
to show her
someday.

Johnny promised.

We turned back to Jonah
and he was asleep
with his mouth open.
It was just like Jonah
to stop the show
with the audience begging
for more.

It hasn't happened again,
but that's fine.
I think it's greedy
to expect a miracle
twice.

Gun Safe

When the day is cloudy,
the river is dark.
You can't see below
the surface.
When it's windy,
the river has waves
that rush past
in a hurry,
thousands of little waves
in a race
to the ocean.

Today it's cloudy and windy.
I take my hair
out of its ponytail
and let it fall in my face.

Your hair is even longer,
Clay says.

Yours, too.
Are you letting
it grow?

Clay touches his hair.
Did you know that hair
grows about half an inch
a month?

New hair pushes out
the old hair, like teeth.
You can use hair
to test for toxic chemicals
and heavy-metals exposure
as far back
as six months.

It doesn't surprise me
that Clay
is performing an experiment
on himself.
Using his hair
to check the levels
of Bugz Away chemicals.

I didn't ask you three things about hair.
And I remember you telling me
that Marie and Pierre Curie
experimented with radium
and died of radium poisoning.

Actually, Clay said,
Pierre Curie died when he fell
under a horse-drawn cart.
But yes, it did make them sick.

I do have a question for you, Clay.

Okay.

Sometimes there is no way
to find out what you need
without just asking.

Where is Gwen's FIREARM?

Clay trails his hands in the river
like me and Rainie.
What is it about the river
that draws people to it?

Dad locked it
in the gun safe he got
from his brother.
Sometimes she sleepwalks
at night
when she takes her sleeping pills
and he was worried.

GUN SAFE?
That's a thing?

Yes, a cabinet to
lock up guns,
keep them safe,
so to speak.
To show the judge
he's being responsible.
Even though Dad's lawyer said
he won't bring it up
at the trial.

Dad was never going to
give them up.
He keeps the key
to the gun safe
on his key chain.

So their family
has a lawyer, too.

The Three Things game
got us in the habit
of being honest
with each other.

Right now,
I think I'd rather
have heard
a white lie
from Clay.

Not how his father
is pretending
to be responsible.

I reach out and touch
a piece of his hair.
It feels dry and warm
in my hand.
It doesn't feel like
a science experiment.

O Man

In the stupidest mistake
ever,
the Oxygen Services Home Delivery truck
turns into
Number 24
instead of
Number 23.

Gwen comes out
(in her bathrobe)
frantically waving
the truck
away.
Does she think
O
is contagious?

The man who carries
the O machine
into the house
asks us where we want to put it.
It comes with twenty feet of
tubing
and makes a rumbling noise
and a hissing sound
when it's turned on.

It's like a magic trick—
the O machine
pulls O
out of the air
and sends it through
the plastic tubing
right to Jonah.

The man also brings
green metal canisters of O.

These are portable—
good for short trips
or outings, he says.

Like Jonah would be packing
a lunch
of O
for on-the-go.

When you use O,
you need another machine.
I call it Fire Alarm.
It screeches when Jonah's O
is low.

Bad timing.
Mom comes home
when the O man
is still here.

What's all this?

Mom stares at the O machine
like it's a piece of furniture
that was delivered
by mistake.
Her finger is rubbing
a tooth again, and
an *ugg ugg* sound
comes out of her mouth.

The O man looks
startled.

It's your oxygen
concentrator, ma'am.

Hmm, Mom says,
and turns her back on it,
the way she did
when her parents
came to visit.

I'd hear her tell Dad,

I'm not gonna ask them to leave,
but I don't have to like
them being here.

White Noise

The school counselor
invites me in
again,
to review the results
of my audiology screening.
There is a little machine
on his desk,
smaller than the O machine,
and quieter,
making a whooshing noise.

What's that machine called?
We have a machine at home
that sounds
a little like that,
but louder,
I tell him.

The counselor squints
at the machine.

This?
It's just a white noise machine.

White noise?

I never imagined noise
as a color.

For privacy, Liv.
Anyway, your results
showed excellent hearing abilities.

Yes, the woman told me.
I hear as good as a bat
or a dog or something,
some animal.

So what is next?
Colleges do care about
sophomore-year grades.

It's not like there's money
for college.
And I've been thinking,
I'd like to do something
different—
something
with my hands.

I tap the top
of the counselor's
wooden desk.

The counselor looks down
at my hands.
For a counselor,
he is slow to understand.
Then he does.

YES YES, HANDS-ON,
the counselor says
really loud,
like he's figured me out.
I check
to see if the
white noise machine
gets louder
when he shouts.
It doesn't.

I can look into that.
See if there are any spaces
available
in our tech programs.
Do you have a
personal preference, Liv?
Automotive technology
Welding
Electrical
Construction
Culinary arts
The programs are geared
toward work in those fields.
And of course there is not
just hands-on training,
but also an academic component.

I tap the desk again.
If I knew Morse code,
I could tap out

my answers,
help him understand.

Hmm.
Automotive, maybe.
I am pretty good with
machines.

And just to prove it,
I reach out and turn off
the white noise machine.

Rooms

After the accident,
after Jonah came home,
we all switched rooms.

Jonah's room off the kitchen
is tiny.
Dad said it was
a pantry
or summer kitchen
or woodshed—
something
old-timey
that got turned into a bedroom.

Jonah's room was too small
for the nurses
and machines,
so he got the living room.

Mom and Dad's room
upstairs
is the big one
facing the street
and Clay's house.

Mom wouldn't sleep
in that room

anymore,
so she took mine,
in the back of the house,
the one that looks out
over the river.

You can see the train tracks
that run along the river,
though no trains
run there anymore,
and you can see
the sky over the river,
and when the leaves fall
in winter,
you can see the river.

In our backyard
there are wooden steps
going down
the steep bank
to the river,
but the path to them
is all overgrown now.

I'm glad Mom
has the river
instead of Number 24.

I have Jonah's little room
downstairs.
When the nurses need me,
I don't have far to go.

Daredevil

After the accident
everyone had the same question.

Did Jonah do it on purpose?

They said to Mom,

*Can you tell me about your son
and why this might have happened?*

At first I thought
Mom wouldn't answer,
but then she did.

*Because he's a teenage boy.
Because he didn't think first.*

*He never had time for thinking,
even as a baby.*

*Not when he tipped himself
out of his crib
headfirst.*

*Ran straight into the swings
at the playground.*

Tried to jump out of shopping carts.

Cut his head open
sledding into a tree.

I didn't mention
the other things—
the ones Mom
doesn't know about:

Walking the metal railing
of the train bridge
over the Kennebec.

Falling through
thin ice
in spring.

So impatient
to start his big life,
to make people laugh,
to see what would happen.

Doing anything
for a dare.

So afraid
he'd be stuck
in Maddigan, Maine,
for the rest
of his life.

No

Mom could teach
the school counselor
how to say NO
with one word.

Liv, he says,
I'm afraid those involved
raised concerns
about the vocational programs
we discussed.
It was mentioned
that a certain degree
of attention
is needed
to ensure safety.
Unfortunately,
the consensus
was that it is not
a good fit
right now.

Mom would have just said
NO.

I feel a little sorry
for the counselor.
He doesn't
look me in the eyes.

That's okay, I say,
I've got some
independent projects
that are taking up
a lot of my time
these days, anyway.

This cheers him up.

Oh, really.
What kind of projects?

Well,
for one,
I am studying the
Kennebec River,
and then
there is party planning
for Jonah's birthday.

The counselor looks
down at his desk again.

I see.
I see.

Logs

If Dad were here,
he'd like my
Kennebec River
independent study.

I would ask him
about the logs
on the bottom
of the river.

If they've been
lying in river water
all this time,
why aren't they rotted?

Is it something
about the water
that does that?

It's like the logs
are in a time machine
down there.

When they're brought
to the surface,
the whole world
has changed.

The Nurses Talk about Me

From Jonah's little pantry room
off the kitchen,
I hear the nurses talking.
It is dark out
when Johnny comes
and Vivian gets ready to go.

I always leave my door
open a little.
I like how the light
from the kitchen
shines into the room.

Johnny and Vivian
talk about Jonah—
his numbers, his machines,
his sounds.

Then I hear my own name—

Liv . . . way too much . . .
responsibility . . .
what kind of a life?
what kind of mother?
hey, I think it's her birthday
the same week . . .
let's do it up right . . .

The small animal
inside me
I didn't know
was there,
is there.

Wanting
Wanting
Wanting

I stop myself
from calling out—

Hey guys,
just because I wear
Hello Kitty pajamas
doesn't mean
I want a Hello Kitty–
themed birthday.
Ditto for
unicorns.

I like cake
but honestly,
I'd rather
cupcakes.
Some people think
trick candles
are fun—
but not me.

I think now I understand
how Rainie feels
when she wants
something.

Vivian leaves
and the house
is quiet,
except for Jonah's
machines.

I know
it's just a birthday
and I'm not a kid
anymore.

But I'm glad
I heard them,
so I can practice
my surprised face
for Jonah's party.

Crossing the Line

A deal is a deal
and I made a promise
to Gwen.

And she made a promise
to me.

I wait on the line
for her.
Good thing it's a
DEAD END,
or I'd be
run over
by now.

Gwen limps to the line
on crutches.
There is an Ace bandage
around one foot.

Sorry,
I tripped on the stairs
and turned my ankle.

I don't know
what she's sorry for—
for being late to the line

for tripping
for hurting her ankle.

But I do like hearing the word
Sorry
come out of her mouth.

Your gun is in
the gun safe.
Your husband
is keeping it
safe.
Because of the sleeping pills
you take.

Clay told you that?

Gwen takes a step forward—
forgetting the line
forgetting the crutches
forgetting her hurt ankle.

She sways,
like she is about to topple,
and I grab her
in my arms.

Even though she is shorter
than me,
she is heavier than she looks.

Her face is on my shoulder,
her arms are around me,
her voice is in my ear.

Clay doesn't have it.
He doesn't have it.
He doesn't have it.

This feels like a
hug.
Mom is not a
hugger,
and Jonah can't
hug back.

Gwen steadies herself.
I hand her the crutches
that fell.

You wanted to know
where the gun was.
Now you know.
And don't forget
our deal.

I look down at the road.
I realize this time
we both crossed the line.

Fudge

I wait
for the
FOR SALE
sign
on Clay's lawn.

No sign
appears.
No moving van
comes and
loads the
Halloween decorations
from the attic,
the Bugz Away
jackets,
the GUN SAFE
and drives off
DEAD END.

I would miss Clay,
but we'd always have
the river.

Then I see Gwen
on the line.
Only one crutch
this time,

something shiny
in her other hand.

When I get closer,
I see that the shine
is made of
aluminum foil.

The thing that's
the strangest—
Gwen is smiling.
A real smile.
An almost hopeful smile.
Clay has the same space
between his top front teeth.

I didn't forget the deal,
Gwen whispers
into the air
between us.

I tried,
I really did,
Clay even took my side,
but my husband won't do it.

I want to say
that the deal was
LEAVING,
not
TRYING TO LEAVE.

Gwen's eyes
are wet now.

Clay talked to me.
He said he was
proud of me.
I made you this.

Gwen holds out
the shiny aluminum package.
It's a perfect square.

In geometry
that means all sides
are equal.

Definitely not true.

Another thing they
don't teach
in geometry—

Even when you can't see
any sides,
there are sides.

I take the square package
from her.

Fudge,
Gwen says.

Fudge?
I ask.

Yes, chocolate marshmallow fudge.
I made it.
For you.

You made it.
Thank you,
I say.

You're welcome.
Let me know how you like it.

I don't know why
we are repeating
everything we say
to each other.

It seems like
we both need to be
very clear
about what is happening.

Gwen made fudge.
She made it for me.

She gave it to me.
I took it.

We both know
FUDGE is not
moving away.
But it's the best
Gwen can do.

Beavers

If I could be one animal,
it would be a
beaver.

I've seen them
on the river.

I've seen the lodges
they make,
that look like
big upside-down nests
made of branches.

I like the way
they use their
teeth and paws—

to chew things down
in one place,
and build them up
in another.

I decide they
can be part of my
independent project.

The next time
we are at the river,
I speak before Clay
has a chance.

Ask me to tell you
three things about beavers.

Tell me
three things about beavers,
Clay says.

I hold up First Finger.
They can close their nose and ears,
and draw a special clear membrane
over their eyes,
when they are underwater.

Second Finger.
Beavers can create their
own wetland habitats.

Third Finger.
I think their lodges
look like big upside-down
bird's nests.

Third Finger
is more a feeling
than a fact,

but I think Clay would agree
that feelings
can be facts, too.

I was going to say,
for Third Finger—
A beaver takes only one mate,
which it keeps for life,
but I changed my mind.

I didn't know
you knew so much
about beavers,
Clay says.

You're not the only one
with facts,
I tell him,
I'm doing an
independent project.

On beavers?

No, on the whole river.

Great topic, Liv,
Clay says.

*Gwen made me
fudge,*
I tell him.

Clay puts a hand
on my shoulder.

*I know.
Thank you for
taking it.
You don't have to
eat it.*

*Why shouldn't I
eat it?
I love fudge.*

I turn so we are
face-to-face.
He keeps his hand
on my shoulder

Can you smile?
I ask him.

*Smile?
Like this?*

*No, with your lips open,
like a real smile.*

Clay smiles with his lips open,
for just a second.
Long enough
for me to see
the space.

Thanks,
I say,
and he is nice enough
not to ask
why.

Lawsuit

I find papers
on the kitchen table
from Mom's lawyer,
full of lawyer words.

"Action for Loss of Services:
Parents of a minor child
may maintain an action
for loss of the services
and earnings of that child
when that loss is caused by
the negligent or wrongful act
of another."

What services is he talking about?
Taking out the garbage,
finally, after Mom starts screaming
about it?
Helping put away the groceries
by seeing if he can throw the bags of chips
and paper towels into the cupboards
from across the room?

And earnings?
Does Mom's lawyer think Jonah's summer job
at the Dairy Whip
would have paid our bills?

"Negligent Entrustment of a Firearm:
Where the entrustor is held liable for
violating a duty of care.
Leaving a weapon where a minor could access it.
For negligence because a breach of duty
provided access to a dangerous
instrumentality."

I don't know why he writes "minor"
rather than "Jonah."

Or why he calls it a
"dangerous instrumentality"
instead of a gun.

Hurricane Chaser

Dad's job
as a millwright
at the paper mill
was a good one
for Maddigan.

It came with all the things
Mom doesn't get at
Tractor Barn—
Health insurance
Dental insurance
Vacation days
Sick days.

Before the mill closed
Dad would describe
the different jobs
to Jonah.

Pipe fitter
Electrician
Crane operator
Paper machine operator
Running the coater
Breaking up logjams

No thanks, Dad,
Jonah would say,
I'm thinking
hurricane chaser
or
smoke jumper
or
raptor rehabilitator.

Dad thought Jonah
was just being Jonah—
out there and funny—
but I knew
when Jonah said
hurricane chaser
he could picture himself
flying directly
into the eye
of a storm.

Is that how it is in families?
One child who stays.
One child who can't wait
to go.

When the mill closed,
Dad stopped telling Jonah
about the jobs.

He'd watch Clay's father
pull out of the driveway
of Number 24
in his Bugz Away van,
and say,

Now there's a smart man—
he's his own boss,
and as long as there's bugs
around, he's got himself a job.

French Braids

Most nights now,
Jonah needs
O.

Rumble Rumble Whoosh
Rumble Rumble Whoosh
The O machine
puts me to sleep.

Then Fire Alarm
wakes me—
EEP EEP EEP
and I go into Jonah's room.

Phoebe is working tonight.
She has a French braid
on each side of her head
going into one long braid
down the back.

Jonah just had a little dip—
he's back to baseline.
Sorry it woke you.

Jonah is having
more and more
"little dips."

Does Jonah hold his breath
to set off Fire Alarm
and get our attention—
or is he trying to see
what it feels like
to give up?

Since you are awake, Liv,
can I ask you
some things
about the birthday plans?

The little animal
inside me
dances.

Sure, ask away,
I say.

So, Jonah's birthday
falls on a Wednesday
and we were thinking
it would be easier
to have the party
the Saturday before,
so everyone
could come.
Plus, I checked,
and your mom
has the day off.

That sounds like
a good idea,
I agree.

I don't say,
By the way
Saturday is also my sixteenth birthday,
because I suspect Phoebe
already knows that.

Now, about food,
we could give Jonah
a little taste of cake,
or at least the frosting.
What sounds good to you?

Well . . .
I pretend to think
about this one.

Jonah likes vanilla cake
and vanilla icing
for his birthday,
I tell Phoebe.

I suppose you do, too?

No, actually I'm more of a
chocolate-cupcake double-
chocolate-frosting person,

but get whatever most people
want,
I say.

Hey, did you do that yourself—
those braids?
I ask Phoebe.

Yes, with three daughters
I have a lot of practice.
Do you want me
to braid your hair?

Sure.

Phoebe finds a brush in her bag,
takes her stethoscope off,
and hangs it on the end
of Jonah's bed.

She gets a chair from the kitchen,
brings it into Jonah's room,
and sets it in front of her
for me.
Jonah keeps sleeping.
Fire Alarm is quiet.
O whooshes and hisses.
Phoebe brushes and brushes,
her hands pull and weave,
twist and braid.

I sit on my own hands
to keep them from reaching up
and touching.
I want them to be
surprised.

It feels strange but good.
Sitting in one place.
Nowhere to go.
Nothing to do.
Someone else's hands
besides mine
at work.

Ghost Town

In the winter,
no one cuts ice
on the frozen river
anymore.

The huge icehouses
filled with sawdust
are gone.

No trains run
across the metal
train bridges
high above the Kennebec.

After the mill closed,
Dad got upset
when someone wrote
in the newspaper
that Maddigan
was a *ghost town* now—
so many stores
out of business,
so many houses standing
empty.

Do I look like a ghost?
he said.
But the way he acted

going from room to room
to room,
staring out the windows—
was a little
ghostlike.

The first week he was laid off,
Dad tightened the loose doorknobs
in the house,
replaced the noisy fan
in the fridge,
and rebuilt
the snowblower motor.

He didn't talk about the machines
he'd worked on
in the shut-down mill anymore.
Except once,
when he found out
they'd be auctioned off.

I have no idea who'll buy them,
where they'll end up,
he said,
it could be anywhere
in the world.

Three Things about Hunter

I met a guy
at the soup kitchen,
I tell Clay
at the river.

It's warm enough that
I don't need my winter coat.
I'm wearing black leggings
and one of Dad's old work jackets
with the paper mill logo
on the front.

You might know him.
Hunter.
He's a sophomore, too.
He's homeschooled,
but he also goes to school.

Hunter?
That's his name?

Just 'cause his parents
named him
Hunter
doesn't mean he
hunts.

You were at the
soup kitchen?

For a punishment.
It's a long story.

I do know Hunter.
He's okay.
His mom predicted the last time
the river flooded the banks.
It probably saved some people's lives.

I didn't know that,
but he's got five
brothers and sisters.
I don't know how many
of each
or their names.
And his parents
are hippies.

Hmm, Clay says,
I wonder if some people
are like animals
and can tell when the weather
is changing—
if they can feel the
barometric pressures.

Hunter can also
play the fiddle,
I add.

Sounds like
we're playing
Three Things about Hunter,
Clay says.

Hunter,
I say his name again
just to show Clay
I don't care
what he's called,
can play the fiddle,
so I invited him to play at
Jonah's birthday party.

This is the first time
I've said the word
Jonah
to Clay
since the accident.

This time,
it's Clay
who takes off
and leaves me
alone at the river.

I'm not sure if it's because of
Hunter
or *birthday party*
or *Jonah*.

Mom

When I see
Number 24
from Mom and Dad's
big upstairs room,
it looks like
just a house.

One of many
on DEAD END,
not there to
remind us
of what happened.

Just a roof,
walls,
windows,
a door,
a pear tree
on the front lawn.

I wish Mom's view
of 24
could be
like the hawks'
that fly high
over the river.

It feels like
the higher up
you go,
the less everything
matters.

Schedule

My schedule
is the same
every day.

World history
English
Chemistry
Lunch
Geometry
Spanish

Spanish
is my favorite,
because half the class
doesn't know
what the teacher
is saying, either.
So I fit right in.

Jonah's schedule
is mostly the same
every day, too,
but sometimes the nurses
and I
switch it up,
and we don't tell Mom.

Mom acts like the
schedule police.

Mom believes
in the schedule.
It's posted on the
refrigerator.
It's her new religion.
It's the one thing
she can control.

It's not like Jonah
is a machine.
He's not going to
run out of gas
and be stranded
on the highway
if Food Truck is late.

If he's sleeping,
why wake him up
to do a "treatment."

We like to let Jonah
sleep in,
take a break,
do something new,
change it up.

After all,
Jonah has to eat the same food
every day, and
doesn't get a say
in what happens
to him,
unless we help him
have his say.

Jonah has faces
and sounds
that mean different things.
If you're watching
and listening,
he will tell you
what he wants,
what he doesn't want.

I think
the Schedule
is Mom's way
of caring for Jonah
without watching
or listening.

What We Have to Say

Mom's lawyer wants Jonah
to appear
at the trial,
so the judge or the jury
can see his *condition*.

Clay will have to
tell
what happened
in the attic.

Clay's father
will answer questions
about his *firearm*.

Dr. Kate will speak
about Jonah's
needs and *care*.

I have to be there, too
but I don't know
why.

I worry what my hands
might do
in the big Headwater Courthouse,

or if I'm asked a question,
whether I will be able
to hear what is said.

I suppose Gwen
will be there, too.

Mom's lawyer
wants a judge,
and not a jury,
to decide who's
at fault.

He said that's because
it could be hard
to find jurors
here in Headwater County
who believe that there
should be any rules at all
about what they can do
what they can't do
with their firearms.

Clay's father's lawyer
could ask for a jury trial, himself—
but he won't,
Mom's lawyer said—
because he's afraid
of what a jury might decide
if they see Jonah.

Three Things about the Kennebec

Clay must know
about the trial, too.
His father's lawyer
might have told him
what to wear,
like our lawyer
told Mom.

What does he mean by
"conservative dress"?
Mom said.
Maybe I can find a
nice skirt and shirt.

Did his father's lawyer
tell Clay to wear a suit
and cut his hair?

I don't ask.
I want things
back to normal
at the river.
Our new normal,
Clay and me.

I like what you did
with your hair,
Clay says.

They're French braids.
Phoebe did it.

Phoebe?

I forget Clay
doesn't know about
our world of nurses—
Vivian, Johnny, Phoebe,
Jess, Lila.

A friend,
I say,
which is not really
a lie.

I don't know if the
word *nurse* would make Clay
walk away again.

I apologize,
Clay says,
for leaving last time.
It wasn't fair
to you.
I'm glad Hunter is playing
at the birthday.

This is so Clay,
not only doing the right thing,
but doing it the right way.

It's okay.
Would you like to hear
three things about the Kennebec?

Sure.

First Finger.
The Kennebec River is about
one hundred seventy miles long.

Second Finger.
It starts in Moosehead Lake.

Third Finger.
It ends in the Atlantic Ocean.

That is going to be a great report, Liv,
Clay says.
Here the river is right in our
backyard,
and I didn't know where it came from
or where it went.

I look out at the eddy,
first upstream where the water
comes from,

and then downstream,
where it is moving
toward the ocean.

I think about how right Clay is.
You can think you know something
so well,
but never know it all.

Dad

All Dad's clothes
are still in the closet and dresser
in the big upstairs bedroom
no one sleeps in.

Some days now,
especially cloudy days,
I take something
of Dad's
and throw it
in the river.

On gray days the river
fills with clouds,
and if it wasn't for the line of trees
on the banks,
you wouldn't know what was sky
and what was water.

It's hard to tell
if the clothes will sink or float,
or if the water will carry them away
downstream.
I got the idea from Rainie
letting the special-deal
necklace go.
Some part of her knew
it wasn't hers to keep.

It might be a sock
or T-shirt
or a hat.

One day,
when Mom is ready to donate
his clothes
to the Thriftee Thrift Shop,
there will be hardly
any left.

Blee-ah

Now that the weather
is warmer,
the nurses want to take Jonah out
in his wheelchair
for walks.

Vivian is excited
for Jonah to get some sun
on his face,
to feel the wind,
to hear the birds,
and, I suppose,
to smell what is left
of the paper mill smell.

It takes a long time
to get ready.
We have to take O,
in case.
Suck-It-Up
hangs in a bag
behind Jonah.
Food Truck is running,
so Vivian puts that
in Jonah's lap.

We find a coat and hat
that Jonah hasn't worn

since last winter.
Vivian buckles him in.

We didn't have the money
to build a wheelchair ramp,
but Vivian and I
each take a side
of the wheelchair
and lift Jonah
down the three cement steps
to outdoors.

Jonah blinks and blinks
at the sun.
The driveway is bumpy
and Jonah bounces
with each bump.

Vivian pushes the chair
and I walk ahead
to watch what Jonah makes
of the outdoor world.

Blee-ah Blee-ah Blee-ah,
Jonah says.

Vivian and I both laugh.
This is a new sound
for Jonah.
Something he sees or hears

or feels is
Blee-ah

We don't know what *Blee-ah*
means,
but Jonah's eyes are wide open,
taking in the sun and the breeze,
laundry blowing on someone's porch,
a dog barking behind a fence,
the sound of a truck turning onto
DEAD END.

I'm doing a *Blee-ah* dance for Jonah
spinning my arms in circles
in front of him,
when I see that the truck
says *Bugz Away*.
Jonah is focused on
Blee-ah
and doesn't turn his head
when Clay and his father
drive past.

That's the way
DEAD END works—
only one way in
only one way out.

Trust Your Hands

Rainie and I go
to Hunter's house
on Saturday
to hear his fiddle music.
He wants me to pick songs
for Jonah's birthday.

I invited Piper,
but she said,

I heard they raise goats.
Goats can transmit
a lot of diseases.
One is Q fever,
and you can get it by
breathing the infectious particles.

"Q fever" sounds like
a made-up disease,
but I don't say that
to Piper.

Justine is busy with an all-day
DIY facial
she read about.

On the way there
I wonder about Hunter's

brothers' and sisters'
names.
Are they variations of Hunter,
like Sniper or Shooter?
Or are they hippie names like
Gatherer and Gleaner and Solstice?

Hunter introduces Rainie to his mother.

I love that name. Rainie.
Why do you look like you want
to cry?

I don't know. I wish I did,
Rainie admits.

And this is Liv,
Hunter tells his mother,
pointing to me.

Hunter's mom
has red hair too, and her
eyes are dark
with specks of light,
as they look into my eyes.

Yes, Liv, what a good girl.
What a good, good girl.

Not really, not always, you'd be surprised.
My hands get me in trouble,
I blurt out.

It's as if Hunter's mom's
eyes hypnotized
us into the truth.

She looks straight at me
and says,

Sure they do, Liv.
But trust your hands
and they'll lead you
where you need to go.

Little kids run in and out of the room.
They are playing a chasing game
where the chasers and the chased
seem to change places in an instant.

What are your brothers' and sisters'
names?
I ask Hunter,
ready to meet brother Target
and sister Bull's-eye.

Hunter claps his hands—
One two three—
and the kids stop running.

Okay, guys,
time for introductions.

Hunter goes around the room
and as he comes to a sib
he raises their hand
in the air.

These are my twin brothers—
Sunrise and Sunset.
This is Little Lima Bean,
Pretty Parsley,
and last but not least,
Sweet Sunflower.

I cover my mouth,
trying not to laugh
at all the hippie names.

Hunter turns to me.

Nah, just kidding, Liv.
You thought we all had
granola names, right?

Little Lima Bean points to Rainie.

Yeah, her—she's the one
got a funny name—
Rain.

I'm Hunter after my
grandfather,
Hunter says,
and tells us the real names
of his brothers and sisters,

but although I can see
his mouth moving,
I can't hear what he's saying,
because I am thinking hard about
what Hunter's mom said—

Trust your hands
and they'll lead you
where you need to go.

Do my hands know something
I don't?

How far will they lead me
and what will I find when I get there?

Music

Rainie is sitting
next to Hunter's mom,
who is showing
Rainie her necklace.

This stone is amber.
Some people call it the
stone of courage.

It's beautiful, Rainie says.

Then I see Hunter's mom
take the necklace off
and put it over Rainie's head.

Rainie holds the deep-yellow-orange
stone to the light.

But it's yours. You shouldn't
give it to me.

Hunter's mom
puts a hand on the place
where her own heart beats.

Take it.
I have all the courage I need
right here.

Hunter claps his hands again, three times.
It must be how you get people's attention
in a family that big.

This song is called "Swallowtail Jig."
Tell me what you think.

And he tucks his fiddle
under his chin
and starts playing.
I can't tell which is moving faster,
his bow or his fingers.

Pretty Parsley and Sweet Sunflower
join hands and dance in a circle.
Twins Sunrise and Sunset
disappear outside.
Little Lima Bean stands there
sucking her thumb.
Rainie holds the yellow pendant
to her own chest.

I'm glad Rainie has the
stone of courage,
but still, I look around
for what else might find
its way into her hands
or her bag.

Justine's stepmom, Brigitte,
is sure
the fountain pen
that was on the desk
in their office
was there *before*
Rainie came,
but not after.

And while we're on the subject,
Brigitte said to Justine,
*not to be picky
or point fingers
at your friend,
but I'm sure
some of the Hershey's kisses
in the serving bowl
are missing, too.*

Really,
Justine said to
Brigitte,
*you count the
chocolate kisses?*

Weight

One day the nurse Lila
is sick,
no one can fill in,
and Mom has to work,
so I stay home with Jonah.

The nurses showed me
how Jonah's machines work,
even the new ones—
O and Fire Alarm.
Vivian says I'm a natural.

I probably inherited that skill
from my father.
Jonah doesn't have as many machines
as they had at the paper mill,
but I know how to keep
them all running.

Sometimes it snows
at the end of April in Maine
but today is warm and sunny.

I dress Jonah
and move his
wheelchair right up
next to the bed.

A fact about ants
that Clay might know—
they can carry ten to fifty times
their body weight.

Ants will carry dead ants
out of their nests, but
sometimes ants carry
other live ants.
This is called
"social carrying behavior."

I'm not an ant,
but by watching how the nurses
move Jonah,
I've picked up some ant-like
abilities.

Especially since Jonah's Trapeze
for cranking him up
out of bed
is broken,
and a new one
hasn't come yet,
it's good that I've got my own
"social carrying" skills.

First I swing his legs
off the bed,

then I put my arms
under his arms
and pull him toward me
until he is sitting up
at the edge of the bed.

Then I do what Johnny calls
"the pivot and shimmy."
I carry Jonah's weight
for the quick few seconds
it takes me to stand and turn him
right into the wheelchair.

There's an amazing split second
in the middle of the pivot,
when I can't be sure
if I'm holding my brother
or he's holding me.

I'm getting stronger
by lifting Jonah—
from the bed to the wheelchair
from the wheelchair to the bed.
His weight feels lighter and lighter
as I get stronger and stronger.

It's like one of those
science rules
Clay loves—
one thing goes up—

the other
goes down.

I put his sunglasses on,
buckle his chest harness
and his seat belt,
and bump him backward
down the three front steps
by myself.

A ribbon of river shines
between the houses
on DEAD END.

I don't trust the wheelchair
on the slatted metal dock,
but the cement boat ramp
slopes gently to the eddy.

I take Jonah's sunglasses off—
like the big reveal.
The whirlpools in the eddy
are lit up by the sun.

Still holding the wheelchair,
I lean my head against Jonah's.
What do you think, Jonah?
See the river.
Remember the river?

Blee-ah Blee-ah,
Jonah says.

Ah, I thought so,
I say.
I knew you wanted to see the
big, beautiful Blee-ah.

Words

I know the trial date
is coming closer,
because Elinor is taking Mom
shopping this weekend
for "conservative court clothes."
I am thinking they should be
black and white
to remind the judge
she is there to decide
who is wrong.

Mom hasn't said no
to the hot casseroles
Elinor brings on Sundays—
enough for us
and the nurses.

I think the lesson Elinor learned
at the soup kitchen
was how to help someone
without it feeling like help.

When Mom's car is gone,
Gwen comes to the line
with more FUDGE—
white chocolate, peanut butter,
chocolate mint.
Her ankle is better

and each time,
she reaches across the line
with both arms
to hug me.

Mom doesn't know
where the fudge comes from.
She thinks a shy fudge fanatic
in Maddigan
is being neighborly.

Also, there are more
letters to the editor
in the paper.
Mom is getting frustrated
by so many
"stolen newspapers."

The next time
I meet Clay at the river,
it is still warm out.

His hair is in a ponytail.

*Is that your new look
for the trial?*
I ask Clay.
This is the first time I've said *trial*.
So many words that are hard to say—
*Jonah, nurses, birthday, Hunter,
mother, father, brother,*

and *trial*.
But we both realize
it can be harder
not to say them.

Yes,
Clay answers.
His knees are bent
up to his chest
and his long arms
are wrapped tightly
around them.

He looks like an astronaut
in a space capsule
on a launchpad,
a ball of anticipation
and dread,
ready for takeoff.

Did you know,
Clay asks me,
*that the word
trial has the words
liar, rat, rail, tail, ail, tar, and lair in it?*

I guess we both
have *trial* on our minds.

I trace the word *trial*
in the dirt next to the dock,
and scratch new words
with my finger
into the ground,
until I find ones
for Clay.

True,
I say,
but also art and air and trail.

You're right.
Clay sounds relieved,
as if I've reminded him
of some basic science fact
like gravity.

Good luck, I say.
I'll be there, too.
And so will Jonah.

I can tell no one told him
the part about *Jonah*
being there.

Ah,
he answers.

What I learn
from watching Clay

by the river today—
things can feel like your fault
even when they're not.

When the trial is over,
Clay says,
it will be your birthday.
What do you want
for your birthday?

I have no idea
when Clay's birthday is,
but he remembers mine.

The little animal inside me
hops around
waiting for my answer.

I don't have a clear membrane
that closes over my eyes,
or a way to seal off my nose
and ears,
but still, I want to go down the
middle of the river
like a beaver.

Clay nods his head,
as if he understands perfectly,
and maybe he does.

Toothache

Mom is making
little hurt whimpers.
Not like Jonah's
big moans.
She pushes her fingers
into the side of her cheek,
as if she can push away
the pain.

What's the matter?
I ask her.
Mom is dressed for work
in her red Tractor Barn shirt.

This tooth.
It was only hurting
once in a while.
Now it's
all the time.

The nurses say
I have good hands.
I wish my hands
could heal,
like it happens
with miracles.
I would put my hand
on Mom's cheek

and watch the pain
go away.

If my hands could heal,
people would come to me,
and I would never turn anyone
away.
Over and over
I would watch the pain
leave their body.

Let me see,
I say,
and surprisingly,
Mom opens her mouth.
Here,
she says,
putting her finger
where it hurts.

I don't need her finger there
to see the problem.
One tooth has a hole
that is black.

Yeah, that looks bad.
What are you going to do?

Mom whimpers again,
a quiet
ooh.

It's almost worse
that she's trying
not to make noise.

I guess it's got to get pulled.
Then I'll have a space there.

We don't say
what we both know.
It would cost more than a day's pay
to pull the tooth
if we had a dentist.
There's no money for
new teeth
to fill the space.

Can I see it again?
I ask Mom.
Maybe it's loose?

Mom opens her mouth,
and one of my hands
gently holds her chin,
and the other reaches—

GRABS THAT BLACK HOLE
OF A TOOTH
AND YANKS IT OUT

AAAARGGHHH

Mom screams once,
and the pain is gone.

She holds my good hands
in hers,
and cries with happiness.

I give Mom a dish towel
for her mouth,
and I throw the
rotten little stone
of a tooth
in the trash.

I want to tell Hunter's mom
she was right.
I trusted my hands,
and they showed me where to go.

PART TWO

Bangs

With the trial coming,
Maddigan is divided—
like our DEAD END
invisible line.
The line starts
in our town
and keeps going.

It's not a straight line.
It curves back and forth,
in and out,
crossing right through
houses and apartments,
over the river,
through the woods,
and down the interstate.

I stop hiding the newspaper
from Mom,
because now Jonah
is on the front page
of the paper
that's for sale
at Tractor Barn.

It's a photo of Jonah
pole-vaulting
at a high school track meet

where he placed first.
It's taken at the moment
in the air
when his legs are on one side
of the bar
and the rest of his body
is on the other side.

There's a photo
from Facebook
of Clay's father
in an orange vest
with a hunting rifle.

Mom irons her
court outfits—
navy-blue skirt/
pale-pink shirt,
brown skirt/
pale-yellow shirt,
gray dress/
black sweater.
If the trial
goes more than
three days,
she'll start over with
navy-blue skirt/
pale-pink shirt.

Elinor painted Mom's fingernails
pale pink
to match her day-one outfit.

Her boss is letting her
take the days off
without pay.

In a way,
it's a good thing
Mom's so busy thinking
about the clothes.
It's less time thinking
about what might happen
in the courtroom.

Mom's lawyer
has a talk
with me about
Fashion Week
"courtroom etiquette."

No shorts, no hat
No flip-flops, no sunglasses
No ripped jeans
No gum chewing
No food or drink
No name-calling
Cell phone off

He pauses a moment,
then asks me:

Any questions, Liv?

What kinds of questions
does he think
I would have about
ripped jeans or
name-calling?

I didn't ask to play
Nine Things about Courtrooms—
unless you count
food and *drink*
separately,
then it's *Ten.*

Yes, I do have a question.
What about bangs?

Bangs?

Mom's lawyer moves
the papers
in his open briefcase
as if there might be *bangs*
under them.

Yes, bangs.

I take a scissors
out of the junk drawer,
rake out the pieces
of my hair in front
with my fingers.
and chop them into long
BANGS

right in front of
Mom's lawyer.

Mom shrugs her shoulders.
She may not understand,
but I guess she figures
it's my hair
to style.

Mom's lawyer closes
his briefcase,
and reaches a hand
out to me
for the first time.

I don't take it.
I am busy fluffing
my BANGS.

I can't wear a *hat*
or *sunglasses,*
but with bangs

over my eyes,
I don't have to see anything
I don't want
to see.
And it makes it hard
for anyone
to see
me.

Sides

If I could understand
what Mr. Sommers
is saying in geometry class,
I would ask him
if there are ever
more than two sides
of a line—
say, in some alternate geometric
universe.

Because when it comes to Jonah
appearing in court,
there are many sides.

Appearing is a strange court word,
since its opposite is *disappearing*.

Some of us want him to appear.
Some want him to disappear.

For once, me and Mom's lawyer
are on the same side.

Mom's lawyer wants Jonah
to *appear* to help win his case.

When I take Jonah for walks
on DEAD END,

it's easy for Clay's father to
pull the curtains
or look away when he's driving
the Bugz Away van—
to make Jonah *disappear* from sight.

In the courtroom I will make
a slit in my bangs
to watch Clay's father
when Jonah *appears.*
If he looks away,
I hope the judge will notice.

There is a Team Meeting
about Jonah's appearance
in court.

There are lines dividing the nurses
and Dr. Kate.

Lila and Phoebe worry
about crowds of people
coughing on Jonah.

Dr. Kate listens
to the nurses
but says there is
no medical reason
for Jonah not *appearing*
in the courtroom.

All his equipment is portable,
even O,
she says.

I am not ashamed of Jonah
or his dent
or his feet turned inward
or his legs that will never stand
or all the equipment we need
to keep him alive.
I heard *Lip* and *Blee-ah*.
I heard the sounds of Jonah
calling from the place
we cannot reach him.

He is my brother.
He always took the leap
over the abyss
without thinking,
and always made it across—
until now.

Let them see it all.
Let them hear what Jonah
has to say.
Let them try and blame Jonah
for being Jonah.

Johnny and Vivian
and Mom and Elinor
and Mom's lawyer and I
will *appear* with Jonah.
There will be six of us there
on Jonah's side.

Dr. Kate

Dr. Kate doesn't leave
when Team Meeting is over.
She takes a seat next to Jonah's bed.
First she looks at his machines,
then she looks at Jonah.

She puts a hand on Jonah's forehead,
as if she's checking his temperature,
but she leaves it there.
Jonah closes his eyes.

It looks relaxing
to have a hand on your forehead,
so I put my own hand on my forehead
under my bangs
and it makes me close my eyes, too.

When I open them,
Dr. Kate's hand is still on Jonah's forehead.
Jonah's eyes are closed
and so are Dr. Kate's.

This is the first time I've had a close look
at Dr. Kate.
She has bangs too,
but they are short and straight,
not long
like mine,

and hers have some
silver hairs in them
I didn't notice before.

When she opens her eyes again,
it's as if touching Jonah
put a spell on her.
She doesn't look at Jonah's machines.
She stretches her arms and yawns.

Whew, I didn't know I was so tired.

Then she looks at me strangely.
I can tell she is wondering
what is different
about me.

I don't tell her
it's my bangs.

My son turns ten next month,
Dr. Kate says to me,
and I understand exactly
what she is saying.

We both watch Jonah.
Dr. Kate puts a hand on Jonah's chest.

*Does your brother often have this kind
of breathing?*
she asks me.

*You mean stopping
and then starting again?*
I ask. That's how I think of it.

Yes, she answers.

*He's been doing it for a few days.
It mostly happens when he sleeps,*
I explain.

It reminds me
of when Jonah would practice for
our river game
Last One Up.

We'd jump from
the high bank
out into the river
and see who could stay underwater
longest.
Jonah and Clay and their friends,
me and Rainie and Justine.
Piper watched from the bank,
because of all she knew about
water-borne protozoans.

Jonah was always the last one to surface.

He used to train at home.
Holding his breath, letting it out,
holding his breath, letting it out,

timing himself
again and again.

Thank you, Dr. Kate says to me, *thank you*,
like Dr. Liv has given her the answer
to some great medical mystery.

On the Record

If you follow the river
downstream,
you will get to the dam
in the town of
Stoppard,
where the Headwater courthouse is.
That is where we will go
for the trial.

Below the courthouse
is the empty woolen mill
that was built on the banks
of the Kennebec.

Five stories high,
the long brick factory
is full of windows
that are mostly broken.

My grandmother worked there
as a loom weaver
from the age of ten
until it closed,
making woolen blankets
and cloth for coats.

Some people want to turn the empty building
into luxury apartments,

because of the river view,
but the soil
and the water
are contaminated
from the chemicals and dyes.
Clay could probably name
the chemicals
if I asked.

In the spring they open the
giant floodgates of the cement dam
to let out
the spring rain
and ice melt
that fills the river.

And the rush of water
is so loud,
no matter what you say
or how loud you shout
your words are swallowed up
into the air.

I'm sorry the spring rush
is over,
because there's no chance,
if the Headwater courtroom windows are open,
that the words spoken there
will disappear.

Even if they did,
Mom's lawyer says there will be
a court reporter
taking down every single word
before it has a chance to
escape.

He doesn't think
I will be called to testify.
But if I do,
it will all be on the record,
he says.

I'm guessing Clay's father's lawyer
told Clay the same thing.
I've always known Clay
to tell the truth,
whether he was
"on the record"
or not.

The Night Before

The phone has been ringing all week
since the trial date was announced
in the paper.
Mom's lawyer says that
if we answer the phone
and we're asked a question
about Jonah or Clay's father
or guns,
we need to say
"No comment."

Mom is afraid she won't sleep
during the trial,
so Dr. Kate gives her a prescription
for a few little pills.

When it gets dark,
Mom takes half a pill.
She offers me the other half.
I say *No thank you.*
I don't care if I can't sleep tonight.
Since Jonah came home
from the hospital,
I've found that, in fact,
not-sleeping
makes me more awake.

Maybe that's my new special animal
talent,
like Hunter's mom being able to
predict storms and floods.

There's a knock at the door
and Johnny lets Rainie in.

She stands there rubbing her amber
"stone of courage"
between her fingers.

My father dropped me off.
He won't let me miss school
to go to the trial,
but I can stay over with you tonight.
Where's your mom?

Asleep.

How's Jonah?

He's asleep too. But he's good.

It surprises me
how true the words feel.

Rainie walks farther into the house
than since before the accident.
She drops her backpack

on the floor,
and peeks under the aluminum foil
of the dish on the counter.

Help yourself to some casserole.
There's also fudge in the fridge.

In her usual Rainie way
that's so familiar to me,
that drives Mom crazy,
Rainie takes a plateful of casserole,
spilling some on the counter,
leaves the casserole uncovered,
pulls off three paper towels at once
to use as a napkin,
tastes a corner of the fudge
with the refrigerator door wide open,
decides she likes it,
takes another plate for her fudge,
and settles herself at the table.

So, who's the bald dude?
Rainie jabs her elbow in the direction
of Jonah's room
where Johnny went.
Is he Jonah's bodyguard?

That's Johnny.
He's one of Jonah's nurses.

Oh, where's the one who did your braids?

That's Phoebe. She only works Tuesdays.

Maybe I can come some Tuesday
and she can do mine.

I see that for Rainie,
and maybe me, too,
the lines are blurry
between nurse, bodyguard, and hairdresser.

What's with all that?

Rainie points her fork
in the direction of my face.

You mean my hair? It's called bangs.

If you say so.
Rainie raises her eyebrows
and we both laugh.

I give Rainie the bed in Jonah's old room,
and I lie down on the floor next to her,
on top of a scratchy woolen mill blanket.
I can hear the humming of Jonah's
Food Truck,
the whooshing of O,

and the loud chirping of a cricket
that found its way into the house.

Then something draws me upstairs
into my parents' big empty room.
I look out into the dark at Number 24.
Clay is standing at his window,
the dark shadow of his body
silhouetted by his desk lamp.
When he sees me,
he puts a hand flat against his window.
I put my hand flat to our windowpane
and we stand there like two aliens
communicating
from separate spaceships.

Back in Jonah's room,
I am kept awake,
not by thinking of the trial tomorrow—
but by thinking about how sometimes
the universe
sends you just what you need—
right when you need it—
the gentle sound
of Rainie's breathing,
Clay's hand.

Headwater Courthouse

Outside the courthouse,
Mom's lawyer explains
that we will be wanded
by a security officer
to check for metal.

Even us? I ask him.

For the first time
he looks annoyed
by what I've said.

*Yes, Liv, everyone who goes into
the courthouse today.*

I think maybe he is nervous.
After all, he is working on "contingency,"
so if he doesn't win,
he doesn't get paid.
Whatever money Mom gets,
he gets one-third.
If Mom gets nothing,
he gets one-third of that.

The security officer's black wand
has a name on it
spelled out in neon-yellow letters—
Garrett.

He tells me to put my arms out
and waves GARRETT
over me and Mom
and Mom's lawyer.
Nothing magical happens.

I'm not wearing any "metal."
My court outfit is—
green leggings,
gray skirt,
Jonah's yellow track jersey
with "CARRIER" on the back
dressed up with a green scarf.
No nail polish.

Jonah is coming separately
with Johnny and Vivian,
in a van that can carry him
in his wheelchair
with his machines.
He will get upstairs
to the courtroom
in an elevator.

We walk up a set of stairs
and on the wall
is a sign:

NOTICE:
FIREARMS PROHIBITED
IN THIS COURTHOUSE

I am glad I thought to hold
Mom's hand
on the way up.

The courtroom has
four tall windows on each side,
pale-blue carpet,
seven doors
(one in front with a red-and-white EXIT sign over it),
wooden desks with microphones,
lots of wooden benches and chairs.

In some ways
it reminds me of my geometry classroom—
there is a blackboard up front
and the ceiling lights have bugz in them.

Mom's lawyer directs us
to sit on the left side
of the courtroom.
Mom sits at a table
next to him.
I sit on a bench
right behind them.

I see Clay
sitting next to his father
on the right side.
I can tell
by how still his head is
that he has his invisible

astronaut helmet on.
Gwen sits on Clay's
other side.
Their lawyer sits next to
Clay's dad.

There are two benches
full of people
behind them.

Elinor comes in
and sits next to me.
In the benches behind us,
our cheering section has
a few neighbors
from DEAD END,
a man from Tractor Barn,
and some people
I don't know.

Like in the *Wizard of Oz*,
the judge suddenly appears
from behind a curtain.

The judge's outfit
is a long black robe
like a wizard
or a Halloween witch.
She looks younger than Mom,
and her hair is pulled back
in a tight bun

so when she looks out
at the courtroom,
she doesn't miss
anything.

I feel her
notice me
for just a second
and move on.
In that second
she shows her superpower—
to heat
up my face
with her eyes.

Someone says
All rise
and we stand up.
Then the judge says
Please be seated
and we all sit down,
and the trial begins.

Jonah

I am watching the few live flies
crawl around in the
ceiling lights
when Jonah is wheeled in
through a door in the front
of the courtroom.
There is instant silence
and all heads, even the judge's,
turn to look at him.

I see what they see—
a skinny teenage boy with
light-brown hair and pale skin,
his head held to the support behind him
with a Velcro strap across his forehead.
A rubbery chest harness
holding his body in place in the chair.
More Velcro holding his feet in place—
in bright white never-used sneakers.
A dent on the right side
of his head.

Vivian pushes the chair
and Johnny wheels the portable O.

I also see what I always see—
my brother Jonah,
as Elinor told Mom,
caught in the belly of the whale.

Jonah's eyes are wide open.
This is only the second time
he's left Maddigan
since he came home
from the hospital.

The first time,
his Food Truck hookup
came out
and when the nurses
couldn't get it back in,
he went by ambulance
to the hospital and back.
Not much of a field trip.

Suddenly,
Jonah's whole body stiffens
and stretches,
his head twists against its strap,
and his raspy voice sounds out
in the courthouse,

KUH-LAY KUH-LAY KUH-LAY
KUH-LAY KUH-LAY

Jonah looks straight at Clay
and there's no mistaking
what word he's saying.

Almost as if he's being ejected
from his shuttle
at warp speed,
Clay is at Jonah's side.

Hey, Jonah, how ya doing?

KUH-LAY KUH-LAY

Yeah, Jonah, good to see you, too.

Jonah looks so astounded
to see Clay,
I wonder if he's been thinking
that whatever happened to him,
worse had happened
to Clay.

Clay's father stands up
and starts shouting at Clay.

CLAY, CLAY, what are you doing?
CLAY, get back here right now.

At one point,
both Jonah and Clay's father
are calling Clay's name
at the same time.

The security officer
is right there next to Jonah.
Another security officer
speaks to the judge.

Mom's lawyer looks around at the chaos
and whispers to Mom,
but Mom is not paying attention to him.

Even if the word Jonah said is
Kuh-lay
and not *Mom*,
it shows her
he is in there.

She is staring at Jonah,
and then she is calling him
by his name
for the first time
since the accident.

JO-NAH, JO-NAH, JO-NAH

NO, STOP IT, PLEASE STOP, PLEASE STOP,
Gwen cries out and covers her eyes.

I can't tell
who she's talking to—
Jonah, Clay, Clay's father, or Mom—
because everyone is yelling at once.

I go over to the right side
and stand in front of Gwen
and clap my hands,
GWEN (clap)
GWEN (clap)
IT'S OKAY. (clap)

I know it's rude
to clap your hands
in someone's face,
but my hands
are inspired.

Gwen uncovers her eyes.
All right, all right, thank you, Liv, she says,
and lets out a big breath.
I can feel her reaching out to me
like we are meeting
on the invisible line,
then remembering we're
in the courtroom.

When I turn away from Gwen,
I see that my handclaps
got everyone's attention,

because they are all
staring at me and
Gwen.
I push my bangs up
and stare back at them.
Clay has a look
of wonder
on his face.
Clay's father's face and neck
are red.
Mom turns her face
away.
Even the judge
is staring.

The judge pounds a wooden gavel
on her table
and announces that
everyone gets twenty minutes for
recess.

I want to see counsel in chambers NOW.
She points a finger at Mom's lawyer
and Clay's father's lawyer.

Vivian and Johnny turn Jonah around
and wheel him back through
the door
he came in.

It may not have lasted long,
and definitely didn't go
according to plan,
but at least Jonah had
his day in court.

Courtroom Decorum

After Mom's lawyer meets with
the judge,
his face is red.

He scolds us—
for speaking out of turn,
walking across the courtroom,
clapping.

There's such a thing as
courtroom decorum.
This judge will be deciding
your case,
he says.

Mom has some of her hard look
back,
and answers him,

May I remind you that YOU
are working for US.

I air clap for Mom
behind his back.

And another thing,
Mom says,

Jonah is NOT returning
to this courtroom.
You can use the video
you made
of him,
if you like.

Mom's lawyer
looks down at the floor.

Very well. That's your call.

Yes, it is,
Mom answers.

If you'll excuse me,
I'll be right back,
Mom's lawyer says,
and exits through one of the three
back doors.

It's just me and Mom.
She shakes her head at me.

GWEN?

Mom draws out the word
like it's the longest one
in the dictionary.

Gwen makes the fudge,
I tell Mom.

Recess

I look at the big court clock.
I have seven minutes left
for recess.

I run down the stairs
past

NOTICE:
FIREARMS PROHIBITED
IN THIS COURTHOUSE

past GARRETT and his
security officer
and out the side door
of the courthouse.

The parking lot is full.
I see a bumper sticker
that says:

"Prayer is a way to get to heaven—
trespassing is faster."

There is a TV news truck
and people with microphones
yell out to me—

Is Jonah coming back?
Is that his jersey
you're wearing?

No comment,
I answer.

I go around to the river side
of the courthouse.
Two hawks are circling over
the water,
round and round,
then gliding
on air currents,
the ragged tips of their wings
outstretched.

I imagine myself up there with them—
a colorful hawk in
green leggings and Jonah's yellow jersey—
the other hawks curious but friendly.

I spread my arms out
and can feel the wind
beneath them
wanting to lift me up.

Next time I see Clay
by the river,
I'll tell him

I'm having second thoughts
about being a beaver.
If I was a hawk,
I could follow the river from its
beginning in Moosehead Lake
to where it meets the ocean—
no dams or sluices to
block my way.

Witness

Mom's lawyer calls Clay
to the witness stand.
He stands there
as still as a wall.
His ponytail
hangs just below the collar
of his white button-down shirt.

The judge turns to Clay
and says,

Would you please state your name for the court.

Clay LeBlanc

Could you please spell your first and last name.

C-L-A-Y L-E-B-L-A-N-C

Will you raise your right hand, please.

Clay raises his right hand,
exactly as he did last night
in his window.

Elinor looks over at me
when my right hand goes up, too.

Do you solemnly swear that the testimony
you are about to give will be
the truth, the whole truth,
and nothing but the truth,
so help you God?

I do.

Please be seated.

I put my hand down
when Clay does.

Watching Clay,
there's something I realize.

He wants to be up there.
He's been waiting
for this chance.
He doesn't know what
will come of it,
but he has to do it.
Just like in the game
Three Things,
when you answer
is when the truth
surprises you
by coming out.

I also see what his parents
and the judge
don't understand
about Clay, the scientist.

The Tin Man
in *The Wizard of Oz*
had the biggest heart of all
but didn't believe it
until the Wizard
gave him the proof
of the ticking clock.

Clay believes that
the facts
will show
what is real,
what was real.

Firearm

Maybe I trusted
too much in

FIREARMS PROHIBITED
IN THIS COURTHOUSE

but I notice
for the first time
what is on the desk
in front of Mom's lawyer
with a tan tag tied to it,

and I shut the curtain
of my bangs.

I must make a funny noise,
because Mom
and Mom's lawyer
turn toward me.

When I was little,
I would cross my eyes
to see double,
and that skill
comes back to me
in the courtroom.

I see one gun/two guns
two guns/one gun/two guns
as my eyes cross
and uncross.

Seeing one gun,
the gun that made Jonah
who he is now,
scares me.
Seeing two guns is just weird.
So I practice seeing two guns.
And I quiet the harsh sound
in my throat
by lifting my eyes—
through the slits
in my bangs—
back to Clay.

Clay

Mom's lawyer
is the first to speak.

Clay, we have the record
of what you told the police,
and your deposition.
But I'd like you to
tell the court,
in your own words,
what happened when
you and Jonah Carrier
went into your attic.

The way Mom's lawyer
says this,
it makes it sound like
"the court"
is a person,
one giant person
with huge listening ears.

If it is possible
for Clay to sit up
even straighter,
he does.

My mom asked me and Jonah to go up in the attic
and get down the box of Halloween decorations.
She has separate bins marked for each holiday
Valentine's Day
Easter
Fourth of July
Halloween
Thanksgiving
Christmas
that she stores up there.

It is so Clay
to list the holidays
in order.

When we got up there,
I went to find the Halloween box for Mom.
Then I heard Jonah say,
Lookee what I found on the windowsill.
When I turned around,
he was holding the gun.

Clay looks past Mom's lawyer
like he is seeing it all happen.
He takes a deep breath
and at the end of the breath
he makes a sound.

I look over at the woman
who is recording the trial,

and her fingers are still moving
over her black recording machine.
I wonder if there is a special button
for the sound Clay just made.

I said to him,
Jonah, put it down.
It could be loaded.
You know my dad.

Mom's lawyer walks closer to Clay
in the witness box.

Why did you say that, Clay?
Did you know it was loaded?

Through the spaces
I made in my bangs,
I see Clay's eyes
jump to his father,
but Mom's lawyer moves
to the right,
so that he's blocking
Clay's view of his father
and his father's view
of Clay.

No, I didn't know for sure.
But I told Jonah,
my dad always says

What good is a gun
if it isn't loaded?

OBJECTION, hearsay.
Clay's father's lawyer gets to her feet.

Mom's lawyer stands up, too.

Admission of a party opponent, your Honor,
he says.

Overruled,
the judge says to Clay's father's lawyer,
because it's the statement of Arthur LeBlanc,
who is the defendant, it's not hearsay.
I want to hear what the boy
has to say.
Please continue,
she says to Clay.

Clay clasps his hands together,
and stares
down at them
for a few seconds
before he speaks.

Then Jonah laughed and twirled the gun
around his fingers.
Is this what you call a six-shooter, Clay?
He tried to twirl it around in a circle
over his head.

Then he stuck it in the front of his pants,
and said,
All right then, I got it safe in my holster, Clay,
oh ye of little faith.

I take a quick peek
through my bangs
at Clay's father's lawyer.
She is on the edge
of her seat.

I said to him,
Jonah, why don't you just put it back
where you found it.
And Jonah said,

Clay, you know I am a master at the game of chance.
WHO defies the odds by performing amazing feats
of daring?
WHO climbs the cell phone tower barefoot?
WHO falls off the roof and doesn't even get a scratch?

When Clay says the word WHO,
he says it just like Jonah did,
even bouncing his head
with each WHO.

Then I asked him
to give me the gun.

But he didn't, he wouldn't.
He laughed, and said,

You really think your daddy would leave
a loaded gun where itty-bitty kiddies like us
could find it?
And blow our little brains out.
Then he took it out of his pants
and pointed it at the side of his head.

All the sound
except Clay's voice
has been sucked out
of the courtroom.
I can almost hear
the flies
moving in the lights.

Everyone waits
for Clay
to speak.
Even the court reporter's fingers
are frozen in midair
over her machine.

There was a shot then,
so loud, so loud,
I didn't know what had happened.
When I opened my eyes,

it was Jonah,
not me,
on the floor.

Clay covers his own eyes,
takes a breath
that is loud enough
to be heard
by "the court,"
then uncovers them.

Mom's lawyer
waits a moment
before he speaks.

Clay, do you have any idea
why your father's loaded gun
was on the windowsill
in the attic?

Clay did not need
to take an oath
to tell the truth.

Mom told Dad that squirrels
were getting into
her bird feeder
in the backyard.
Dad said he'd
take care of them.

Thank you. No further questions,
Mom's lawyer says.

Mom turns
to look at me
for the first time
since Clay started talking.

She raises her eyebrows
and shakes her head.
I know exactly
what she's thinking,
because it's what
I'm thinking, too—

Hard as it is to hear,
it isn't worse than
what we had imagined,
and there were a few minutes,
when Clay spoke Jonah's words,
that it felt like the old Jonah
was here with us
in the courtroom.

Cross

Clay's father's lawyer
now has a chance
to "cross-examine" Clay.
It seems to be a way
to kick someone
when they're down—
but that's how it works
in a court.

The lawyer
is a woman hired by
their insurance company.
She is wearing
"conservative court clothes" too—
dark-gray skirt, dark-gray jacket,
and pale-pink shirt
the same shade as Mom's.

I have a few questions for you, Clay,
she says.

You said that Jonah picked up the gun himself?

Yes.

*Did I hear you say you told Jonah
that the gun was likely loaded?*

Yes, but I don't think . . .

*This is a yes-or-no question. Again, did I hear you say
you told Jonah that the gun was likely loaded?*

Yes.

Did he acknowledge your warning?

I don't know what you mean by acknowledge.

*Let me put it another way. Is it true that even after you
    told Jonah
that the gun was likely loaded, and to put it back where
    he found it,
he nevertheless continued to handle this gun that was not
    his?*

Yes.

Thank you, no more questions,
she says.

The judge tells Clay
he can step down,
and Clay goes to sit
in the chair
between his mother and father.

When he is seated, I see
Gwen lay a hand on his shoulder,
the one that is closest to her,
and when she does that,
I can feel Clay's bony shoulder
in my hand, too.

Clay's father,
waiting his own turn
for the witness box,
makes believe
there is nothing but air
between him and Gwen.

Arthur

Clay's father has a name,
besides "Clay's dad," "Mr. LeBlanc"
or "President of Bugz Away Pest
Management."

He spells it for the court.

A-R-T-H-U-R L-E-B-L-A-N-C

A-R-T-H-U-R was once someone's baby.
Did they pick A-R-T-H-U-R because
A was first in the baby name book?
Did they hope their kid would do
great things,
like pull a sword out of a stone,
as easily as I took the tooth
from Mom's mouth?

Mom's lawyer carries the gun
over to the witness box.
I can't see A-R-T-H-U-R without
also
seeing the gun.

Mom's lawyer asks him a question.

Is this your gun?

After that, all I know
is that a membrane grows
over my eyes and ears,
like on a waterlogged beaver,
but it is not clear,
because I can't hear anything
except a wavelike sound,
thudding over and over.
I realize it is not water,
but my own heartbeat.

The back of the bench
is hard and straight
and it reminds me
of the seats on the merry-go-round
at the Maddigan State Fair.
When I was little,
I insisted on the seats
instead of the horses.
I'd tell Dad
I KNEW the horses weren't real.
Of course Jonah had to stand,
not sit,
on the horse's back.
Mom was mad
she didn't get her photo
of me and Jonah
sitting on horses.

I am spinning now
and the room is getting dark,
and I don't have to see anyone
or anything
anymore.

I remember that all I had to eat today
was a slice of fudge,
and I feel myself falling,
and I simply let myself
go.
Then I am moving
through the air,
and I am crying,
Leave me on the merry-go-round,
oh, please
leave me on the merry-go-round.

Maybe I'm not crying
out loud, though,
because no one answers.

When I can see again,
I am in the front seat of Elinor's car.
Elinor feeds me leftover cold
McDonald's fries,
and warm Pepsi,
and they taste so good.

Mom and the security officer
watch me sip the Pepsi
through a straw,
like I'm the most talented person
they know.
I dip a fry in a paper cup of ketchup
Elinor hands me.

I'm fine now,
I tell Mom.
You can go back in.

I'll take her home,
Elinor says.

Go,
I tell Mom,
and she does.

Elinor and I follow the river
back to DEAD END.
The right side
of my head is sore,
in the same place
Jonah has his boo-boo.
Elinor sees me touching it
and wincing.

You hit
the edge of the bench

when you fell,
she says.

When we get back
to Number 23,
Elinor leads me into
the little room
off the kitchen.
I get into bed
and Elinor gives me an ice pack
for my head
and a cup of milky hot chocolate.
She stands there while I drink it,
and takes the cup back.

Try to rest, now, Liv,
she says,
I'll be in the kitchen
if you need anything.

She throws the scratchy blanket
over me,
and it weighs me down.
I hear Dr. Kate and Vivian
talking
in Jonah's room,
and I wonder
why Dr. Kate is here,
when it's not
Team Meeting.

I never go to bed
without first checking
on Jonah,
but now I lie here
in the middle of the afternoon,
the merry-go-round taking me
round in circles
until I'm asleep.

Snorkel Man

It is getting dark out
when I wake up,
and I am still in my
court clothes.

I hurry to the bathroom.
And when I come out,
Mom is at the kitchen table.

How did it go with Mr. LeBlanc?
I ask her.

Mr. LeBlanc
said he didn't go inviting people
into his attic
to handle his personal property.
And told the judge
HIS son
knows all about
gun safety.

What is happening in court
tomorrow?
I ask her.

The firearms expert
and Dr. Kate are testifying.

Please eat something
in the morning
before we go—
besides fudge.
We need to talk about
one other thing, Liv.

Mom checks the pale-pink polish
on each fingernail.
She is quiet for so long
I think she's forgotten
what she wants to say.
Then she speaks.

Clay is missing.
After the judge
called it a day,
he was supposed to wait
by their car,
while they talked to their lawyer
in the courthouse,
but when they got outside,
he wasn't there.
The police at the courthouse,
couldn't find him, either.
He never came home.
I saw Clay's dad outside
with a flashlight.
It's like he just disappeared.

Why are you telling me this?
I ask Mom.
Do you think I know where Clay is?

Do you?

I don't. I have no idea where he is.

I am distracted by a new noise
coming from Jonah's room.

What's that sound?
I ask Mom.

It's a sleep thing
for Jonah
that came today.
Phoebe can explain.

Everything happened
while I was on the merry-go-round.
Clay disappeared, and
Jonah got a new friend.

I go into Jonah's room.
He's all tired out
after his big trip
to Headwater Courthouse.
He is napping with a
plastic mask

over his face,
and he smells like the lotion
Phoebe rubs on his skin.

Phoebe says that
after Dr. Kate had the talk
with Dr. Liv,
she ordered another machine
for Jonah
for when he sleeps—
Snorkel Man.

When Jonah is down underneath
the river,
holding his breath,
Snorkel Man
blows air
in and out
of his lungs,
one deep-sea diver
to the other.

See how good Jonah's
numbers are now,
Phoebe says.

It's true.
No loud EEKS
or flashing red lights.
Snorkel Man is on the job.

I stretch out on the recliner
next to Jonah's bed.
Phoebe has her hair
in a waterfall today—
it sprays out
from the top of her head
in all directions.

Take a rest, Liv.
I hear you had quite the day,
she says.

It's pretty clear
that everyone has
talked to each other
about my day
in court.
They look at me
like I might topple over
at any moment.

Mom brings me a bowl
of Elinor's latest casserole—
ham, cheese, peas, and noodles—
and a glass of water.
They all want to feed me
now.

Where is Clay?

The little animal inside me
has no manners.
It makes a pouty face.
Its birthday
is coming
and Clay has disappeared.
How will it get its
present?

If Clay is really gone,
who will meet me
at the river now,
to tell me the three things
I need to know?

Where are you, Clay?
Where did you go?
And why?

Truth

The door slams
and I hear Rainie
drop her backpack.
There is a loud rumbling
as a car backs out of the driveway.

Rainie comes all the way
into Jonah's room
for the first time.
She touches her amber
stone of courage.

What's that thing on Jonah?
she asks.

It helps him breathe, Phoebe says.
Snorkel Man, I say
at the same time.

Snorkel Man doesn't answer.
He's busy blowing air—
Whoosha Whoosha Whoosha

*I wish I could sleep
with all that noise,*
Rainie says.

Rainie watches Phoebe
filling up Food Truck.
She walks around the
living room,
looking at Jonah's cans of formula,
his machines, the O tubing
stretched along the floor.

Your father's car is very loud,
I say from the recliner.
Isn't there a law against that?

Since Rainie's father
is a policeman,
she knows lots of ways
people get in trouble.

Hunter's mom dropped me off.
There's a hole in the exhaust
of their car.
She didn't make it loud
on purpose,
Rainie says.

Ah, HUNTER,
I say.

Rainie says,

It's not like that.
I like helping Sara out.
We made goat-milk soap today.

Who's Sara?
I ask her.

Hunter's mom.
Hey, how'd it go at court?
Did the judge make Clay's father
get rid of his guns?

I pretend that Rainie asked me
three things about the trial,
and throw in a few extra.

The trial is not over.
Tomorrow is day two.
There's no decision yet.
Mom's not trying to get rid
of Clay's father's guns.
She's trying to get money
to pay for Jonah's care.

Rainie picks up Zombie Vest
and holds it up to herself
like she's at Walmart
and trying to decide
whether to put it
in her shopping cart.

My dad said that's
what the trial is about—
guns.
But yeah, it must cost a lot
for all the nurses and stuff.

Phoebe raises her eyebrows at me
and smiles
when Rainie says that.

There is something I've learned
in my one day at court—
no matter how plain
you make your truth,
not everyone will see it.

Headwater Courthouse Day Two

You don't have to
sleep on the floor,
Rainie says that night,
and moves over
to make room
for me
in my bed.

I think about
getting up,
and going to the river,
to look for Clay,
but I'm pulled down into sleep
and don't wake up
until the morning
of Day Two.

Sara is there
with her loud exhaust,
to pick Rainie up.

Good luck,
Rainie says,
and runs out the door.
I don't know what
Good luck
she means,
but I say thanks.

Good luck
for Mom and Mom's lawyer
to win?
Good luck
not to pass out
again?
Good luck
for taking away
guns?
Good luck
for a miracle
for Jonah?
Good luck
for Clay
coming back?

Elinor is here
to watch the house.
The phone has been ringing
with questions about the trial,
photographers taking photos
of Number 23 and Number 24,
newspeople knocking on the door.

Mom hands me
a box of cereal
to eat in the car,
like I'm a toddler.

She has on her Day Two outfit—
brown skirt, pale-yellow shirt.

My Day Two outfit:
Jonah's black-and-yellow hockey jersey
comes halfway to my knees—
CARRIER on the back
in yellow,
like GARRETT—
a thin, shiny black belt,
and black leggings.
Above my bangs,
the rest of my hair
caught up
in a waterfall
like Phoebe's.

Today GARRETT and I
are old friends—
he waves at me
and I wave at him—
both of us
black and yellow.

Mom's lawyer
looks even more nervous
than yesterday.
He avoids looking at me.
Even though
"fainting in court"
wasn't on the prohibited list,
I don't think he's happy

with my court behavior
yesterday.

Clay's dad and Gwen
sit in the same chairs
as yesterday,
with a Clay-sized space
between them.

Is there a spray
in Clay's father's truck
that vaporizes bugz?
Would Clay use it on himself,
spraying one
body part
after the other,
timing how long
they take to disappear?
Would he start with his feet
or his head?
Since he has that science mind,
he'd know he needed
to save
his eyes
for last
to see what was gone
or not.

It's a cloudy day and no sun
shines through the tall windows.
It feels cold in the courtroom

and I shiver in Jonah's thin jersey.
When the rain starts,
it's so loud against the windows
and on the metal roof
that Mom's lawyer has to
raise his voice
to be heard.

First he shows
the "before" video
of Jonah
on a screen
up front.
Some of it's blurry
because Jonah is moving—
shooting a puck, pole-vaulting,
catching a baseball in midair.
In the parts where he is still,
Jonah smiles at the camera—
the happy face
that made everyone
like him.

There's one clip
in our backyard
where I'm hiding
from the camera
behind Jonah.
You can see my arms
and my hair

and the Kennebec River
behind us.

That is Jonah then.
This is
Jonah now,
Mom's lawyer says.

And we have Jonah's doctor
here,
to explain what I will be showing
in the video.

Dr. Kate
takes the stand,
and spells her name,
and takes the oath.
She holds her hands together
in front of her
like she is praying,
and waits,
like we all do,
for the movie
to begin.

Jonah After

The screen lights up
right in front of where
Clay's father and Gwen
are sitting.

Mom's lawyer
pauses the film,
to say
how the first image
was taken by the police
when Jonah came into the
emergency room.

His voice is suddenly drowned out
by the pounding of the rain
against the windows.
It's as if all the water in the river
rose up and threw itself
at the courthouse.

Did Hunter's mom, Sara,
predict this?
Headwater Courthouse is old
and this must happen
in big rains,
because when water starts dripping
in the right front corner

of the courtroom,
the security officer appears
with a bucket.

Please continue,
the judge says to Mom's lawyer.

It's easier for me
to listen to the rain
than to Mom's lawyer.

So I do.

It's like tuning
to a different wavelength
on a radio.
I turn the dial
in my ears
to Rain.

Clay's father and Gwen
don't have much choice
where to look
but at the screen.
If they turn their heads one way,
Mom and I
are sitting there.
If they turn the other way,
the judge will see
they are looking out the window

instead of
eyes up front.

Then come videos of Jonah
after his surgery—
in the hospital,
in rehab.
His face says,
"WOW, something VERY BIG
must have fallen on me."

The next thing we see
is the video
of Jonah at home
that the professional videographer
took when I was at school.
It shows Jonah
being fed
being dressed,
all his machines
working hard.

You can see Vivian
giving him meds,
washing him,
pedaling his legs,
rowing his arms.

As we all watch,
Dr. Kate tells the ways

Jonah is a baby now.
Tube-fed
Total care
Nonmobile

I like that the rain
washes away her words.

Apnea
Aspiration
Oxygen dependent
Seizure activity
Partial paralysis
Permanent brain injury

When Mom's lawyer is done
with the Jonah show,
Clay's father's lawyer
gets up.
With her back to the screen,
she speaks to Dr. Kate.

Let me ask you this.
Would you say that there's always
a chance Jonah Carrier's condition
might improve, that new treatments
or medications might mitigate the
severity of his present diagnoses?

The rain comes down harder then.
The security officer checks the bucket

under the drip.
Even with my ears
tuned to the Rain station,
I can't help listening
for her answer.

Dr. Kate looks up at the last frame
in the video.
Jonah is being moved
from the bed
to the wheelchair
in his Trapeze.

I wish that were true,
Dr. Kate answers her,
but in Jonah's case,
I have to say his condition
is considered intractable.

Clay's father's lawyer pauses.
I think she's wondering
how she can look up the word
"intractable"
on her phone
without it being obvious
to the judge.

I don't know
what it means, either,
but I can guess.

Instead,
she thanks Dr. Kate for her time,
and sits down.

I decide that
even if it's still raining,
tonight I will go to the river,
and wait for Clay.

Hair Trigger

I didn't know there were
"firearms experts."
It's not a subject
they teach in school.
Not even in the
"hands-on" programs
they won't let me join.

The firearms expert
doesn't look much older
than Jonah.
He is wearing a police uniform,
and in between answering,
he bites his fingernails.

After he says and spells
his name
for the court,
A-B-R-A-H-A-M B-E-R-R-Y
explains that he first
saw the firearm
after the accident,
when he was asked to
examine it
for the police.

I think Clay would like
Abraham Berry.
He tells the facts
he knows to be true
about the gun.

He doesn't seem to be on
one side
or the other.

No, he answers Clay's father's lawyer,
the Smith and Wesson Model 17 revolver
belonging to Arthur LeBlanc
was not damaged
and it did not have a hair trigger.

Yes, he answers, *my findings are*
that the gun did NOT go off by accident.

That means the gun
can't be blamed
for what it did.

No, he answers Mom's lawyer,
it did not have a trigger lock
or a cable lock,
and there were five more bullets left
in the six-bullet cylinder.

Mom's lawyer asks
the firearms expert
another question.

Were there other firearms
taken from the home of Arthur LeBlanc
that you examined?

Objection, lack of personal knowledge,
Clay's father's lawyer shouts.

The judge turns her
see-through-you eyes
to Abraham Berry.
Arthur LeBlanc previously testified
that other firearms were taken from his home.
Did you examine those?

Yes,
Abraham Berry answers.

I will allow it,
the judge says.

How many other firearms
did you examine?
Mom's lawyer asks Abraham Berry.

There were six other firearms,
he says.

And how many of those
were loaded?

Objection,
Clay's father's lawyer says again,
more quietly this time.

I'm going to allow it,
the judge says again.

Two of the six guns
were loaded.

I didn't know guns
had names,
and numbers.
I didn't know
so many bullets
could fit in
one gun.
I didn't know someone
would have
so many guns.
I have been in Clay's house.
There are three rooms downstairs,
and three bedrooms upstairs.
Does Clay's father have one gun
for each room,
and an extra
for the attic?

No one in the courtroom
has anything left to say.

The judge looks down from her
high seat.
Her X-ray eyes freeze us in place.

Each side to file posttrial briefs
within two weeks, as agreed.
I will take this under advisement.
This court is now adjourned,
she says, smacks her gavel on her desk,
and stands up.

Someone says
All rise,
and everyone stands
as the judge disappears
through the curtain
behind her.

Clay's father and Gwen
immediately get up and leave
out the back door.

What does that mean?
Mom asks her lawyer.

It means she will consider all the facts
and render an opinion sometime
in the coming weeks.

Is the trial over then?
Mom asks.

Yes, it is,
he answers.

Good. Two days' lost pay
is two more than I can afford.
How do you think it went?
Mom asks him.

I think it went as well
as it could.
How it will turn out,
what the judge will do,
I can't predict,
he says.

The ride back home
is quiet
except for the rain,
that is still coming down hard.
Mom has her headlights on.
That's a rule in Maine,
Rainie told me—
if you're using your windshield wipers,
you have to have your lights on.

Now that the trial is over,
Mom says,
I expect that you'll put your attention

back where it belongs—
on your schoolwork.

Mom is concentrating hard
on the rainy road in front of us,
so she doesn't notice that I'm trying
to defrost the foggy windshield
with my laser judge eyes.

I'll take that under advisement,
I answer.

PART THREE

Where Are You, Clay?

Clay is not at the river.
There is no note left
under a rock there,
because I look.
Mama duck swims by,
her babies following
in a row.

I throw one of Dad's
work hats
into the eddy.
Lightweight, it bobs there
on top of the water.
I turn back home
before it sinks.

Clay is not at home.
I see his father leave
in the Bugz Away van
by himself.
No light comes on
in Clay's room,
no hand at his window.

The next day it's me
on the line,
waiting for when Gwen
gets the mail.

Only I can't see the line
anymore,
and I cross over
to the mailbox.

Gwen's not wearing
her bathrobe,
but her sweatpants and sweatshirt
are not much better.
Her hair looks like
she just woke up
and forgot to brush the back.

I don't even have to ask.
She tells me
three things about Clay:

Yesterday,
he cashed all his paychecks
at once,
that he's been holding on to
for five months.
I do the books for the business,
so I saw it.

My brother told me
Clay bought the pickup truck
he had for sale—
paid for it outright.

And before he left the courtroom,
Clay whispered to me,
that whatever happened,
not to worry
about him.

Gwen looks as proud
as if she's telling me
Clay got into his
first-choice college.

Saving his paychecks
Buying a pickup
Telling Gwen not to worry.
I think she is happiest about
Number Three—
her son cared enough
that he didn't want her to worry.
It all sounds like a plan.
A plan Clay never talked about
to me.

Did he say anything else?
I ask.
In the courtroom, I mean.
Before he left?
Like where he was going?
Or what he was going to do?

Gwen studies my face.
She puts a finger
on the place
where I fell.
I stand very still,
waiting.

Oh my, yes,
how could I forget.
He told me to tell you
he's going down the river.

Gwen waits for me
to tell her
what Clay means by
"going down the river."

If I had to guess,
I'd say it means he's
moving on,
letting the current
carry him along.

I think it's her finger gently rubbing
on the place
where it hurts,
like she is trying to erase
the bruise,
that makes me say,

I think it means he's okay,
that he's doing what he needs to
right now.

Even if it's not true,
there's a good moment
there at the Number 24 mailbox
when we both believe
what I say.

When's Clay's birthday?
I ask Gwen,
thinking of my birthday
and Jonah's.

It was last month,
on the fifth.

Oh,
I say.

Here I am wanting Clay there
for my birthday,
and I missed even saying

happy birthday
to him
on his.

Today I have all the questions
for Gwen.

What color is the truck?

Red, I think,
Gwen says.

Now we both
will have our eyes out
for that color.

Jonah

The day after the trial
I stay home from school.

I tell Mom I'm a little dizzy,
which is half true.
If I stare at the end of my nose
with both eyes,
I do get dizzy.

I'm doing what Mom said she wants
me to do—
"putting my attention
back where it belongs"—
and today it belongs
with Jonah.

I still keep the Jonah calendar
in my head,
but I changed the rules
for Good Day/Bad Day.
It doesn't matter
how many of Jonah's machines
lend a hand.
As long as Jonah
doesn't cry
to be set free,
it's a good day.

This way,
there's a much better chance
for a good month.

Jonah's been sleeping
a lot,
Vivian says,
since he went to the courthouse.

Time to wake up, lazy boy.
I hold on to Jonah's shoulders
while I bounce the bed,
so we bounce together.
No time off, Jonah,
not when I'm here
and I need your attention.

Jonah opens his eyes.
Thank you, Jonah,
nice to see those
baby blues.
Here Vivian is thinking
she's not your favorite nurse,
'cause you're sleeping
through her shift,
I tease him.

Jonah's eyes move to Vivian,
where she stands by his bed,
filling up Food Truck.
Jah-Nee,

Jonah says,
with a sidelong glance
at Vivian.

Did you say
what I think you said?
Vivian does a very good
fake-hurt face.
Did you say you liked Johnny
better than me?

JAH-NEE,
Jonah repeats,
louder this time,
and laughs in the way
Jonah now laughs.

It's a cross between
a cough and a gag,
like the laugh is in there,
but it's hard to get it out.

Vivian and I laugh with him,
and Vivian gives him a hug.
When she does that,
Jonah leans his head
into hers,
and I feel something
very private
pass between them.

The little animal inside me
gets throw-something mad.
Jonah teased Vivian.
All the nurses
love him.
Jonah has this world
without me.
Everything is turned
upside down.

I know it's wrong
to feel this way
about my brother,
but the animal is hurt
and won't listen
to reason.

We're all changing places.
No one is who they're
supposed to be.
Gwen understands me
better than Mom.
Sara is the one
who gives Rainie
what she needs.
Elinor is Mom's new
BFF and stand-in family.

Vivian is not just
a nurse
to Jonah.

I know it's true—
but I don't like seeing it.

Vivian's superpower must be
taming wild animals,
because she opens her arms
to include me in the hug.

Then, instead of clawing
at my insides,
the animal lies down
and takes a rest.

When the group hug ends,
Vivian asks me,

Have you seen a ring?
Phoebe lost her mother's ring.
She asked me about it
this morning.
She thinks she took it off
and left it near the sink
when she washed her hands
the other night.
I looked,
but I couldn't find it.
It's a mother's ring,
if you see it,
gold with birthstones
for each of her three girls.

No, I haven't,
I say,
but I'll definitely
keep my eye out
for it.

Rainie, Rainie,
is my first thought,
both of us
with our wild animals.

Birchell

My first day
back in school
after the trial,
it's obvious
that's all everyone's
been talking about.

Someone asks me,

If your mother wins,
are you going to take Jonah
to Disneyland?

No, I answer,
a trial is not a
Make-A-Wish.

Piper and I
are walking down the hall
when we see four boys
standing together.
Boy Number 1
points a finger at his head
and falls to the floor.
Boys 2, 3, and 4
laugh.
When Boy Number 1 stands up,

Piper charges at him and
knocks him back down.

You think that's funny?
Jerk!
she yells.
My feet are rooted
to the floor,
watching the boys' expressions change
when they see me.
Piper pulls on my arm
and turns us
in the other direction.

On line in the cafeteria I hear
Clay's name.

Yeah, he started working at Brann's Dairy Farm,
living in a crappy trailer behind the barn,
milking cows and shoveling shit.

When I get home,
I think about telling Gwen
what I heard,
leaving out some of
the language,
but there's a gun
in our mailbox.

I know it's not real
since it's yellow and green,
and Clay said guns
don't come in colors.
Plus, it's plastic.
But still, it's a gun,
and it's not going to be
my problem.

I slam the mailbox door
and find Mom's lawyer's number
on papers in the house.
If he's hoping to get
one-third
of any money Mom gets,
he can deal with the things
that happen
because of the trial.

Birchell here, he answers.

I didn't know his first name
was Birchell,
but I recognize his voice.

This is Liv, Jonah's sister,
and someone put a gun
in our mailbox,
I say.

Oh my God, Liv,
DON'T TOUCH IT,
he yells over the phone.

I'm not STUPID,
I yell back,
plus it's a toy gun,
you know, yellow and green
plastic.

Does your mother know?
You need to call the police.
They'll come investigate
the scene.
They may also want to keep
an eye
on the house.

You know what, Birchell,
Mom's at work,
and the police are not going to
care what
I say.
Do you think
you could come over
and deal with it?
So the gun
is gone
by the time
Mom comes home.

Birchell drives over
wearing jeans and a button-down shirt.
He's like a centaur,
which we learned in mythology
is half human, half horse.
He is half regular guy,
half lawyer.
Birchell talks to the police
when they arrive.
I stay inside.
I don't care
who put it there
or why,
but before the police leave,
the mailbox
is empty.

*Your mom might think about
getting a post office box,*
Birchell suggests,
*at least until the trial buzz
blows over.*

I brush my bangs to one side
of my see-through-you judge eyes.
I start to tell him that I will take that
under advisement,

but instead my good hand
reaches out and shakes his
lawyer hand.

Thank you, Birchell,
I say,
and I mean it.

Cows

Mom comes home happy.

Guess what,
she says.
*People at work
donated their own hours
to make up for my lost days
at the trial.*

*How was your day
back at school, Liv?*
Mom asks me.

My day was great, too,
I say.
*Hey, what do you know
about Brann's Dairy Farm?*

*I went to school with Bobby Brann.
That farm's been in his family
for generations.
It's right on the intervale there
along the river. Such a pretty spot.
Why?*

No real reason.
I heard some kids talking about it
at school.

I think Bobby's gone all organic,
Mom adds.
No one around here can afford
organic milk,
but there's a market for it
down southern Maine.

This is more conversation
than Mom and I have had
in a long time.

I'm happy too,
that Mom's coworkers
gave her just what she needed.

I remember passing the place
outside of town,
where black-and-white cows
stand in a green field
that goes down to the river.

Dad said intervale soil
is the best there is—
no rocks at all,
because it comes
from the river floods.

I think
milking cows
and shoveling
cow manure
is better than
killing bugz.

And I'm sure
Clay is learning
three things about
organic cows.

Mom is staring at me
like she's trying to figure
something out.

*The police called me
about the mailbox,*
Mom says.

*You don't have to protect me.
I'm your mother.
I'm supposed to protect YOU.*

In that case,
I say,
my day really sucked.

Limbo

I hear Mom on the phone
telling Elinor
that she feels like
she's in limbo
waiting for the judge
to make a decision.

I look up the definition
of the word "limbo."
It's a dance, and it also means
"somewhere between
here and there."
It's a place
where "nothing is clear or certain."
It's also a situation
where "you have to wait
to find out what will
happen next."

I'm in limbo, too
while we wait
for the verdict.

Letters to the editor
fill a whole page
in the paper.

"A win for the plaintiff
could set a dangerous precedent
for our gun rights. The next thing
we know, the government will be
taking the guns right out of our hands."

"The tragic truth is that two boys' lives
were ruined by the carelessness of
one man. No matter what the decision,
everyone is a loser."

"In the end, we are all paying for
the care Jonah Carrier will need
for the rest of his life. And I ask the
question, Who is going
to pay for MY care?"

How can anyone know
that Clay's life
is ruined?

I'm in limbo
watching
for a red truck
that never comes.

Every night,
I wait down at the eddy
alone.
The water is warming up.

It's light out later and later.
There are frogs croaking
and little minnows hiding
in the shadows of the dock.

Jonah's eyes are closed
more and more.
The only voice
that will wake him up
every time
is mine.
It's like he's in limbo too—
somewhere between
awake and asleep.

Suck-It-Up is being
a very good friend.
Lately, no matter what the time,
he's by Jonah's side.

The party is in three days.
The guest list
on the fridge
gets longer
every day.
Dr. Kate is coming
and so is Birchell,
and Hunter and Sara
and all the hippie kids.

I don't feel
"clear or certain"
whether I should
talk to Rainie
about Phoebe's ring.
What can I say?
Please ask your animal
to give it back?

I learn that
I don't like
being in limbo.
Even if it's bad news,
I want to know
now.
I'm not good
at being "between here
and there."

Team Meeting

There's a
Team Meeting
to talk about
Jonah's big sleeping,
all the
"support"
he's been needing,
and the crackly sounds
in his chest.

Jess and Lila think
he has his days and nights
mixed up.

Vivian says,
He seems to be . . . ,
and she looks over at Mom,
ah . . . withdrawing a little.

I know the words
she means to say
before she remembers
Mom is there—
"giving up."

That can't happen,
because then it would be
just me.

Johnny and Phoebe
don't say anything.

I think Jonah is bored,
I speak up.
I'd be bored,
doing the same thing every day,
and, no offense,
I love you all, but
seeing the same people.

When Jonah's O needs stabilize,
we can look into a day program,
Dr. Kate says then,
nodding seriously at Dr. Liv.
There is a stroke-and-head-injury rehab program
at the hospital,
where he could be picked up
and do therapies and activities
during the day.

How old would the other people
be, in these programs?
Mom asks.

I can see she hopes
these programs
will be like a fun summer school
for Jonah,
with other kids his age.

There's a range,
Dr. Kate says.

Everyone in the room,
except Mom,
knows that's not a real answer.

The Fidgets

There's not much room
to pace
in our house
at night.
I can't go upstairs
because Mom is asleep.

The kitchen to my room
only takes two steps.
Johnny watches me walk around
the kitchen.

You know, the best cure
for the fidgets
is getting in the birthday-party spirit,
he says.

Who says I have
the fidgets?

How many times
did you just look
in the refrigerator
in the last thirty seconds?

I thought you nurses
were planning everything—
all the food
and the guest list.

Johnny reaches into the
oversize man purse
that holds his stethoscope,
water bottle, and food,
and tosses me a bag
of balloons, a plastic
hand-pump balloon inflator,
and three packs of folded-up
birthday banners.

What the heck?
I say, holding them all
in my arms.

Dollar-store specials,
Johnny says.

No string for the balloons?

Johnny reaches back into his bag
like Mary Poppins, RN,
and holds up a spool of kite string.

Is Jonah awake?
I ask him.

It's hard to tell,
Johnny says.

I carry all the party supplies
into the living room.

Let's wake him up,
and get him
in his chair,
while we decorate.
Maybe this is his
daytime,

I say to Johnny.

We lift Jonah into his chair.
It feels like he
is fighting us
in a quiet way,
letting his arms hang
and stiffening his legs
on purpose.

I notice Food Truck
is serving seltzer
instead of vanilla milkshake.
That's a first.

Change in menu?
I ask Johnny.

It's Pedialyte,
Johnny explains.
He wasn't tolerating
the formula.

When Jonah is sitting up,
I sit next to him
and start pumping up
balloons.

Blue, yellow, pink, red,
purple, green, orange.

Jonah opens his eyes
to see what we're doing.
I put a green balloon in his lap,
and move his hands
onto it.

Hey, Jonah, I say,
Johnny and I are doing
some middle-of-the-night
party prep.
What do you think?

Jonah smiles at me.
Both sides of his mouth
don't move in the same

direction anymore,
but I remember the before-smile
so well, it's what I see.

Maybe Jonah *was* just bored,
because he's wide awake
for the party decorating.

OOG OOG,
he says,
whenever another balloon
is blown up.

Johnny puts Jonah's
Zombie Vest on him
and switches it on.
Brooka Brooka Brooka
Brooka Brooka Brooka
Zombie Vest shivers.

Johnny starts dancing
around the living room.

I attach balloons to Food Truck,
and tape them to the ceiling
over Jonah's bed.
I even run out
in the dark
and tie some
to our mailbox.

Johnny is right.
Blowing up balloons
and hanging banners
is the perfect cure
for the fidgets.

Surprise

On the morning
of my birthday,
Mom says,

Liv, can you come with me
to the supermarket?
I need to pick up
some last-minute things
before the party.

What things?
I ask.
It looks like there's two
of everything already here.

Uh, uh, ginger ale and
chips.

When I hear Mom's "Uh, uh"
I know it's an excuse
to get me out of the house.

Can we go to the other
Hannaford,
south of Maddigan?
Past Brann's Dairy Farm?

I suppose so,
Mom says.
What's this sudden interest
in dairy farming?
It's hard work
and no benefits.

I've been thinking about
eating more organic food.

Then you might also think
about your education.
I'll bet that judge
in the trial
can drink all the organic milk
she wants.

I pull my hair,
including my bangs,
to the top of my head,
and narrow my eyes
at Mom.

I'll take that
under advisement,
I say.

Mom laughs
at my imitation
of the judge,

and sneaks a look
at the clock
on the kitchen wall.

The organic cows
are out in the green field
this morning.
Someone is on a tractor
putting round bales of hay
out for them.
I can't tell if the person
on the tractor
is Clay
or not.

Can you pull over?
I ask Mom.
*I might know that person
on the tractor.*

Maybe because it's my birthday
and she has the day off,
and she needs to keep me
out of the house,
Mom stops the car
on the side of the road,
next to the fence.

There used to be a set of steps
down to the river,
behind Bobby Brann's house there.

Mom points to a spot
I can't see.

Your father and I, and Elinor,
and lots of the old gang
swam off there.

I want to hear Mom
talk more about Dad,
but I'm in a hurry
to see who's feeding
the cows.

I walk along the fence
until I'm close enough
to the tractor
that I can see
it's not Clay.

The man on the tractor
is skinny and tall,
like Clay,
but he's about
a hundred years old.

He drives the tractor
over to the fence.

Hi,
I call out to him,
I was wondering if Clay is here.
I heard he's working for you.

The man
takes his hat off
and holds it in his hands
for a while
before he speaks,

He's not working for me.
I'm retired now.
He's working for my son Bobby.

It doesn't look to me
like he's retired,
driving the tractor
out there in the sun
in the big field.

Is Clay here?

Your young man
asked for the day off.

The old man's mouth
makes a kind of sneer
when he says "day off."

*Thanks, but
he's not my young man.
I like your cows.
How many do you have?*

*There's thirty-two cows,
ten heifers,
plus the new calves
gonna be born anytime.*

Wow!
I say.
*I've never seen a
new calf.*

I kind of hope he will invite me
to see the new calves
when they're born, but
the old man doesn't say anything.
It's like he's already used up
all his words
for the day.

*When you see Clay,
can you let him know
Liv was here?*

The man bows
his head,
puts his hat back on,
and starts up the tractor.

The whole time
we've been talking
the cows hardly move.
They have everything they need—
the hay, the grass,
and lots of other
black-and-white cows
for company.

I don't remind Mom,
when she buys spaghetti
and tomato sauce,
that we are there for
ginger ale and chips.

Wish Time

When we get home,
Mom hangs back,
so I open the door
first.

Even though I've practiced
my surprised expression,
when everyone shouts
HAPPY BIRTHDAY LIV!
my face freezes
like I've never been
surprised before,
and it doesn't know
what to do.

Then they sing,
while Hunter
plays his fiddle.

Happy birthday to you
Happy birthday to you
Happy birthday, dear Li-iv
Happy birthday to you.

It's such a simple song,
but when I hear it,

it makes me really feel
like it's my birthday.

Hunter's sisters must have heard
"party"
and decided the theme was
garden princess or
fortune-teller ballerina.
Little Lima Bean and Pretty Parsley
are wearing long dresses
decorated with dried flowers,
Sweet Sunflower is wearing a sparkly tutu
and a bandanna on her head.

They are dancing around
with paper plates
full of food.

You're the birthday girl.
Do you want food?
We can get you a plate.
Hunter said we had to be
helpful.

Sure, I say,
I'll have a plate.

What's your favorite?
What's your favorite?

The girls all talk at once.

The kitchen table is covered
with dishes.
The cupcakes are chocolate
with chocolate frosting.
All the foods
are my favorites—
deviled eggs,
sliced salami,
guacamole and blue chips,
nacho chips and salsa.

*I'll have some of
everything,*
I say.
Oooh.
Little Lima Bean
jumps up and down,
like that was the perfect answer.

I look around.
Justine is talking to Mom.
She is waving her arms
and Mom is shaking her head.
Phoebe and Sara
sit next to each other
on the couch

in the living room.
I hear Sara whisper to Phoebe,

Do you feel it?
The shift of energy in this house?
It's very strong.

Hunter's twin brothers
are helping Elinor
arrange a platter of
cheese and crackers.

Johnny clinks a glass
with a spoon
to get everyone's attention.

WISH TIME, LIV,
he says
when the room is quiet.
He puts down the glass and spoon,
sticks a candle in a chocolate cupcake,
and lights it.

I look around for Jonah.
He's in his chair.
For the first time,
Snorkel Man is keeping him company
when he's awake,
instead of just at night.

Johnny sees me notice this,
comes up next to me
with the cupcake,
and whispers,

He was struggling a bit
this morning.
I can take it off
if you want.
He's doing better now.

I shake my head no.
I don't mind having
Snorkel Man
at the party.
It's Jonah's party, too.
He can invite
whoever he wants.

Machines aren't going to
spoil my birthday.
Jonah's friends
are my friends.

I hold my breath,
make my wish,
and blow out the candle.
Everyone yells yay and claps,
like they're sure
my wish will come true.

Ring

Piper is in the kitchen
holding an empty plate.

She points to the platter
of deviled eggs.
*Do you know how long
those have been sitting out?
It's two hours max
at room temperature
for cooked eggs.*

Piper doesn't say what happens
after the two hours,
and I don't ask.
Under the kitchen light
the yellow in the eggs
looks like dried-up Play-Doh.

Too long, is my guess,
I say,
and take the deviled egg off my plate
and put it back on the platter.

Those look good,
I suggest,
pointing to the big bowl
of blue chips.

They do,
Piper agrees,
then comes closer
and whispers
in my ear,
but have you seen
how many people
reached into the bowl?

I hang my arm over Piper's shoulders
and try to walk in her shoes
for a moment,
to feel what it's like
to see germs everywhere.

Let's go listen
to the music,
I say.

Hunter sits in a chair
next to Jonah
playing his fiddle.

Dr. Kate listens to the concert
and eats a cupcake.

The glass doors are open
between the kitchen
and the living room.
We haven't had
this many people

or this much food here
since Dad died.

Look what I found!

Little Lima Bean shouts,
as she crawls out
from under Jonah's bed.

She holds up a gold ring
with three small birthstones,
one for each daughter.

Phoebe pulls Little Lima Bean
and the ring
into her arms,
kissing Little Lima Bean
and the ring,
one after the other.

Harmonica

I relight the candle
in my cupcake
on the stove burner
and bring it over
to Jonah.

I give Snorkel Man
a little time-out.

As I start the song
for my brother,
everyone joins in.

Happy birthday to you
Happy birthday to you
Happy birthday, dear Jo-nah
Happy birthday to you

I bring the lit cupcake
close to Jonah's face
and mine,
so no one can tell
whether it's my breath
or his
that blows it out.

Is it time for presents now?
Don't you want to open

your presents?
Pretty Parsley asks.

Pretty Parsley and Little Lima Bean jump around
next to two piles of wrapped boxes
and gift bags
stacked on the counter.
Someone has separated them
into a pile for Jonah
and a pile for me.

Sweet Sunflower reaches up
to touch the bows and ribbons.
Her purple bandanna
hangs around her neck
and she makes a whistling sound
when she breathes.

Eeeeech Eeeeech Eeeeech
like the wind
blowing through our old windows
during a blizzard.

My gift for Jonah first,
I say,
and take the Thriftee Thrift Shop
harmonica
out of my pocket.

Sorry I didn't get to
wrap it, Jonah,

but it's the thought
that counts,
I joke.
I thought you might want
to make your own music.

I hold the harmonica
to Jonah's lips.

Breathe, Jonah,
breathe a big breath out.

Hum Hum

Jonah makes music,
and when he smiles
there's no mistaking
his happiness.

Encore, Jonah,
I hold it to his mouth again.

Humm Humm

Hunter's sisters applaud
and everyone claps with them.

When Johnny brings over
the first wrapped
present for Jonah,
he is asleep.

I slip the harmonica
into the front pocket
of Jonah's shirt.

Good job, Music Man,
I tell him.

My Presents

This is from me and Sara.
She helped me pick it out,
Rainie says.

Rainie gives me a card
and a small package
the size of my hand,
covered in purple cloth
and tied with what looks like
bailing twine
but I'm guessing must be
hemp
or dried vines.

Underneath the cloth
is a white box,
the kind jewelry comes in.
Inside the box
is a stone
on a chain.

It is deep purple,
gray, and blue green,
depending on how I
turn it.
There are also flashes
of red and silver.

It reminds me of the river
at night
when the moon
shines on it.

It's an iolite sunstone,
Rainie says.
Here, read the card.

I had forgotten
to open the card first,
the way Mom made
Jonah and me do
at our birthday parties
when we were little.

The card says:

"Dear Liv,
The iolite sunstone is a
'stone of the heart,' associated with courage,
great compassion, and bigheartedness.
I think this describes you perfectly.
Sara says it's also thought of as a compass,
meant to guide you on spiritual journeys.
Always your best friend,
Rainie"

Mom was right
about opening the cards first.

I put the necklace on,
and when we hug,
Rainie's stone of courage
and my stone of the heart
touch.

Mom's present to me
is a new sheet set
for my bed.

The receipt is taped to it,
Mom points out,
in case you want to return it.

Why would I want to return it?
I say.
It's perfect.

Piper and Justine
got me a gift certificate
to a hair salon in town,
and a bag of hair clips
and headbands.

Since you're into
changing up your hair
these days,
Justine explains.

Vivian gives me
Superwoman pajamas.

Phoebe gives me fuzzy socks
she knit herself.

Johnny and the other nurses
give me a plastic toy car
with doors that open.
Inside there's a voucher
for the cost of the driver's ed
class at school.

I'm really surprised
at this gift.
I hold the toy car
and the voucher
and thank them
over and over.

They knew Mom couldn't afford
the class,
but they thought
it was important enough
that I be able to drive away from
DEAD END one day.

Birchell gives me a bouquet
of red roses in a vase.

Thank you, I say,
smelling their sweetness.
No one ever gave me
flowers before.

Dr. Kate's gift is at the
bottom of the pile.
The long cardboard box
is not wrapped
or in a gift bag.
There's no ribbon
or card.

When I open it,
there isn't a pendant
or a pair of fuzzy socks.
There's a stethoscope.

The room gets quiet
for a moment,
when I lift it out of its box.

Dr. Kate doesn't seem to care
what anyone thinks about a
stethoscope as a Sweet Sixteen gift.
She speaks to me, ignoring the rest
of the room.

If you're going to be a doctor
one day,

this will be one of your most
essential tools,
besides your mind and your heart
and your hands.

I put the stethoscope
in my ears,
the way the nurses do.

I like how the earpieces
muffle the noise around me,
and I like how heavy
the metal circle on the end
feels in my hand.

When you use a stethoscope,
your ears and your hands
work together.
I put the metal circle
over my heart.

My own heartbeat,
which I've never heard before
is loud
in my ears.

THUMP THUMP THUMP
THUMP THUMP THUMP

My sixteenth birthday party
and Jonah's eighteenth
continues around me,
and I wonder if this is how
a heart sounds
when it's full.

After the Party

When everyone leaves,
the house is the same—
the bathroom sink drips,
there are water stains
on the ceiling,
the wallpaper
curls at the edges.

It's the same,
but it feels brighter.
It's not just all the
balloons and wrapping paper,
and the leftover food—
cupcakes and olives,
salami and chips—
in the middle of the table.
It's something else—
something that didn't leave
when the guests did.

Mom tells Johnny
to go home
instead of working his night shift
with Jonah,
because he's been awake all day
at the party.

What about Jonah's presents?
I say,
sounding like one of Hunter's sisters.

We'll save them for when he wakes up,
Mom says.

Do you need any help with Jonah
before I go out?
I ask Mom.

No. Where are you going?
Mom asks.

Down to the river,
I answer,
but I'll have my phone
with me.

Say hi to the river
from me,
Mom says.

Clay

First I see a red pickup truck
parked in the gravel parking place
near the eddy.
Clay is there,
lying faceup on the dock.
I can't tell if he's asleep,
or if he's studying the
cloudless sky.

There's no breeze out, and
the river looks absolutely still.

I talked to a very old guy
on a tractor this morning.
He said you had
the day off.
He sounded like he's never
had a day off
ever.

Clay sits up and
looks at me.

That might be true,
he says.

So do you like working
with organic cows?
I ask him.

I do,
Clay says,
They're real creatures
of habit.
You have to milk them
the same time,
morning and night.
They really have their
own personalities.
There's one cow
that always tries to kick me.

It's my birthday,
I tell Clay.

I know,
Clay says.
I got you something, but
it's not here.
I have to take you to see it.

I follow Clay
up DEAD END,
around to the back
of our house.

You're taking me to
my own backyard?
I ask.
Then I notice something
different about it.

There's a neat pile of brush
on the ground.
Someone has reclaimed
the overgrown path
down to the steps
that lead
to the river.

I look at Clay.

You did this?

Yes.

Wow! Thank you. That's a nice present.
We haven't been able to get down there
in years.
Dad always meant to do it.

You're welcome,
Clay says,
I checked and the steps are still good.
But that's not your present.
Your present is down there.

Clay points down the steep bank
toward the river.

What could be down there?
I wonder.
Did Clay do all this work
cutting the brush
just to hide my gift
down there?

I walk down the steep wooden steps,
holding the railing,
until I'm on the bottom step.

Tied to the trunk
of an overhanging tree
and floating in the water
is a canoe.
Inside the canoe
there are paddles
and a life jacket.
On the side of the canoe,
in blue letters,
is one word—
LIV.

That's my present?
That's for me?

I turn around to ask Clay.
He comes down and stands
next to me
on the last step.

Yes, I hope you like it,
'cause I can't return it.

I don't just like it,
I LOVE it.

Clay smiles
and I see the space
between his front teeth.

When I asked,
you said that more than anything,
you wanted to go down
the middle of the river
like a beaver.
Now you can go down the river
anytime you want.

I put my arms around Clay.
He has a different smell.
Not Bugz Away chemicals
anymore.
Maybe the smell is organic cows
or maybe I'm smelling
the real Clay.

He puts his arms around me,
and kisses my hair,
then kisses my lips.

I don't need my Dr. Liv
stethoscope
to know what my heart
feels.

Liv, Liv,
Clays says,
and I hear the words
LIVE LIVE.

I reach for the rope
to move the canoe
toward us.

Let's go, Clay.
Let's go before it gets dark,
I say.
Let's go be beavers
on the river.

Magic Lotion

When I get back home,
my arms ache, and
my body feels like it's still
moving down the river.

Mom is curled up
sleeping
in Jonah's bed,
and Jonah is wide awake
in his chair beside her.

It's like he's watching
over her.

I wheel Jonah into the kitchen
and close the doors
to the living room
so Mom can keep sleeping.
Food Truck comes along,
serving seltzer again.

I take Phoebe's magic lotion
with me.
That's what the nurses
call Phoebe's bottle of
moisturizer.
At first they thought
it was a coincidence—

the evenings Phoebe
massaged the lotion
on Jonah's hands, feet,
legs, back, face
before bed,
he slept all night.

Those nights,
there were no
loud cries
for help
waking me.

We still call it
magic lotion,
even though we know
the magic is in the touch.

Another thing I've learned—
touch makes you feel
you're not alone.

I put lotion on
Jonah's arms and hands,
rubbing it in small circles
the way Phoebe does.

Jonah turns his head
to look behind him,
and there's a question-mark look
on his face.

Are you looking for Mom?
She fell asleep on your bed.
I thought we'd let her sleep
a little, and kick her out
when you're ready for bed.

Jonah's eyes still search
the room.

Oh, you're looking for Johnny
or Phoebe.
Mom told Johnny to go home.
He was here all day
at the party.
It's a no-nurse night,
just the three of us.

I take off Jonah's sneakers
and socks, and rub lotion on
his feet, doing each toe
separately.

I wonder if it reminds Jonah
of when he used to stand on
the ground—
the feel of something solid
against the bottom of his feet.

Jonah's eyes move,
to the front door,
to the stairs,

to the windows,
back and forth
over and over,
over and over.

I finally get it.

You're looking for Clay?
I ask Jonah.
You're wondering why
he didn't make it
to the party?

His eyes stop darting around
and settle on me.

Clay's working at Brann's Dairy Farm
in south Maddigan,
and he doesn't get much time off.
But maybe he can come another day.

I can't tell
if this is what Jonah
wanted to know,
needed to know,
or if he's thinking
about all the other friends
who stopped coming
a long time ago,

but when I'm done talking,
Jonah closes his eyes.

Is he imagining
what it's like
to work on a farm?

I finish with Phoebe's magic lotion—
massaging the knots
out of his calves
with my thumbs.

Then I wake Mom
and together
we get Jonah,
already asleep,
back to bed.

PART FOUR

Audrey

Piper texts me,
"Audrey is in the hospital
with asthma.
Caroline and Mariah
really miss her."

I learn that Sweet Sunflower
is named Audrey,
Little Lima Bean is Caroline
and Pretty Parsley
is Mariah.

Sweet Sunflower's whistling,
which sounded like a rusty music box
caught in her throat,
was asthma.

Even Sara,
with her extrasensory powers,
felt a shift in energy, but she
didn't see this coming.

I know how that is—
how the worst thing
is right where you
least expect it to be—
in your lungs,
in your chest,

in the attic
of the house
right across the street.

Liv

The Wednesday after the party
is Jonah's real birthday.
It's also spring break
from school.

The sun is bright
when I go down the steps
in the backyard.

When I see LIV
floating by the shore,
it feels like my birthday
all over again.

I wear my life jacket
because I promised Clay
I would.

Being on the river
is nothing like
looking at it
from land.
The wind blows in my face
on the way downstream,
and rocks the canoe.

The end of my paddle
is long and flat
and I smack it
against the water,
the way beavers
slap their tails
when they're startled.

I stop paddling
to watch a hawk
overhead,
and steer over to the riverbank
to touch a water lily.

The best part of
being on the river
is that there's nothing
that needs to be done
except staying afloat.

I can paddle
or not.
I can let the river
take me where it will,
or I can move forward
so fast
I forget
where I started from.

What Form?

When she gets back from work,
Mom tells me
what Birchell said—
the judge's decision
could come any day now.

In the meantime,
we are still waiting—
waiting to lose,
waiting to win—
and I can't imagine
how either of those
will feel.

I wonder:
If the judge decided
to let us vote
on the verdict,
me, Mom,
Clay's father, Gwen, Clay—
who would win?

Me and Mom
would vote for the money
for Jonah,
and Clay's father would vote
against.
Probably Gwen would vote

against, too,
even though she crossed the line.
That would make Clay
the tie breaker.

I can't guess how the judge,
with her wide-screen eyes,
will vote.

Vivian is moving
out of state.
Lila is taking
a new job.
Jess is going
back to school
in the fall.

Everyone is moving on
with their lives—
except Jonah.
The nurses are family,
then they are not.

Mom asks me
if I've seen a form
that was in the kitchen drawer.

What form?
I ask,
not saying I know
it's Jonah's

Do Not Resuscitate form
she's looking for.

Just a form,
she says,
maybe the nurses moved it.

The paper
might still be folded
in my jacket pocket.
I used it
to wrap a piece of fudge
to take out on the river.

Nuummite

Jonah's presents
are waiting
on the counter
for him to wake up enough
to open them.

Johnny has Jonah sitting up
in bed,
with a wet washcloth
on his head.

What's with the new look?
I ask Johnny.

He's got a fever,
Johnny answers.

EEK EEK
Fire Alarm goes off.

Johnny listens to Jonah's
chest, fiddles with O
and Snorkel Man,
then goes into the kitchen
to wash out syringes,
and draw up Jonah's meds,
and give us some sibling
alone time.

I decide to ignore
all of Jonah's friends,
and pile the wrapped gifts
on his lap.

Jonah, I say,
it's your real birthday today.
Eighteen years old.
You have lots of
presents to open.
Of course,
nothing's gonna be as good as
your harmonica.

I see the harmonica
on the nightstand
and blow into it.

HARUM HARUMMM

Jonah opens his eyes
when I play.
I don't know if it's
from the fever,
but his eyes
are extra shiny,
the way Mom's are
after she cries.

Oooh, look!
I open the first package.
A blue sweatshirt from Mom!

I hold it up for him to see, then
I drape it over his shoulders
so it hangs down in front of him.

I open the next gift.
Oooh, amazing, Jonah!
Another blue shirt from Vivian!
I'm sensing a theme here,
you clothes horse, you!

And I hang the second blue shirt
over the first.

The next present
is from Hunter,
and it's a CD of fiddle music.
I put it in the CD player
for Jonah to hear.

With the music playing,
I open the rest of the birthday gifts.
If you think about it,
it's hard to get a present
for someone who can't eat,
read, walk, or use his hands,
but the gifts are great—

funny movies, more CDs,
squishy pillows.

Jonah also has a card and package
wrapped in orange cloth
and tied with hippie rope.

"Dear Jonah,
This stone is called nuummite but some people
also call it the 'Magician's Stone.'
It's one of the oldest stones on earth,
and came from a volcano. It is supposed
to help you find space and freedom.
Love, Rainie and Sara"

The shiny black stone
hangs from a soft cord,
and when it moves,
gold, green, and blue colors flash.
I put it around Jonah's neck.
The noises he makes
when he breathes
Ratch Ratch Eratch
are louder than Snorkel Man's,
as if Jonah wants
to have the last word.

There you go, Jonah,
all the presents are opened
and you are legally an adult.

Jonah is watching
the Liv Birthday Party Performance
with a face that means
he's humoring me.

I can't joke about all the things
eighteen usually brings—
the right to vote, get married,
buy lottery tickets,
so I say,
Happy birthday, big brother,
I love you,
and lift the cool washcloth
to touch my forehead
to his.

I've learned that
hearing something is good,
but feeling it is better.

Jonah

During the night Mom wakes me.

Liv
Get up
Get up

All the lights are on downstairs.
Mom is dressed,
and Johnny is in Jonah's room
on the phone.

I hear him talking

Yes, number 23
He's seventeen, no, make that eighteen
years old.

Nikki, can you turn on
the outdoor lights
and move the car
out of the driveway,

Johnny calls out to Mom.

What's going on?
I ask Mom.

Jonah,
she says, pointing in his direction.

Jonah's face is a shade of color
you might call blue or gray
or something in between.
His eyes are closed,
his lips are purplish,
and his hands are so dark
I can't even give them a color.

He breathes one long breath
at a time,
with a wait in between,
like he can't decide
whether or not
to take the next one.

Johnny drips medicine
in the corner of Jonah's mouth.

This will help,
he says.
The O is as high
as it can go.
I shut that off—
he points to Fire Alarm—
it just kept alarming.
Your mom asked me to call 911.
The ambulance is on its way.

I hold Jonah's cool hand in mine.
Breath
Wait
Breath
Wait.
I match my own breaths
with Jonah's.
It makes me dizzy to
breathe with him,
and my heart is beating
so fast,
I can feel it pulsing
in my ears,
even without a stethoscope.

There are sirens
in the distance
getting louder.

Mom is in the doorway.

What will they do
when they get here?
Mom asks Johnny.
What will they do?

They may put in a breathing tube
to help him breathe.

I don't say that Jonah
seems to have his own
way of breathing now.

THAT'S NOT WHAT DR. KATE SAID,
Mom screams at Johnny,
she said I could decide.
I could decide
if he got a breathing tube.
I could decide on
life support.
Isn't a breathing tube
life support?

Johnny answers her
in a quiet voice.

Yes, Nikki, it's up to you,
but you asked me to call 911,
you wanted them to come.

I WON'T I WON'T,
Mom comes closer
and screams in Johnny's face,
I WON'T LET THEM TAKE HIM AWAY AGAIN.

Okay, okay, Nikki,
Johnny tries to soothe Mom,
when there are loud knocks
at the door.

Johnny looks at me and Jonah,
and follows Mom into the kitchen.

Breath
Wait
Breath
Wait
Wait
Wait
Breath

I hear everyone talking.
Mom still hasn't found
her inside voice.

YOU CAN LEAVE NOW
I CHANGED MY MIND
I DON'T WANT A TUBE
DOWN HIS THROAT
BREATHING FOR HIM
YOU CAN'T TAKE HIM
DR. KATE SAID
SHE GAVE ME A PAPER TO SIGN
IF I WANTED TO

We don't have to do that,
I hear a woman's fake-calm voice
talking to Mom,
we can just assess him,
put on the monitors,

take a listen,
we can call Dr. Kate,
speak with her.
I can't imagine
how hard this is
for you.

Breath
Wait
Wait
Breath
Wait
Wait
Wait
Wait

I can't see Mom
from where I sit
on the bed
with Jonah,
but I feel the fight
go right out of her.

Wait
Wait
Wait
Wait
Wait
Wait

I finally have to blow out
all the air I've been holding
in my cheeks
waiting for Jonah's next breath.

When Johnny and a paramedic
come in
to check on him,
Jonah is gone.

Johnny lays his hand
on top of Jonah's head.

Fly high, my man,
I will miss you, always,
I hear him tell Jonah.

It doesn't surprise me
that Jonah, the trickster,
wearing his Magician's Stone,
would disappear
when we were all looking.

Cans

When the paramedics tell Mom,
Yes, Jonah died,
she starts throwing things.

She begins with the cans
of Jonah's food.
She throws them out of his room
into the kitchen,
then she opens the front door
and throws them out onto the lawn.
Can after can after can.

When all the cans are gone
from the house,
Mom takes the drawers
full of medical supplies
and dumps them in the garbage.
She pours Jonah's medicine
down the sink.

GET THIS OUT OF HERE
AND THIS
AND THIS
AND THIS
AND THIS
she tells the paramedics
(who've decided their new patient

is Mom),
pointing to O
and Fire Alarm
and Food Truck
and Suck-It-Up
and Zombie Vest
and Snorkel Man.

One by one,
I watch Jonah's friends
leave the house.

When she is done
redecorating,
Mom remembers her manners,
and thanks the paramedics
as if they are moving people
who are nice enough
to show up
in the middle of the night
to lend a hand.

Soul

It's three thirty a.m.
and the lights are on in
Number 24,
but I don't see any faces
in the windows.
I imagine that an
ambulance
parked in the driveway
and Mom's missile launch
of cans
onto the front lawn
makes it hard for them
to sleep.

I feel so strange.
My hands hang there
at the ends of my arms,
with nothing to do
for Jonah
anymore.

He lies in the bed
with no plastic prongs
in his nose
or O tubing curled
behind his ears.

There are no tubes
anywhere.

The room,
with all his friends
and equipment gone,
looks bigger
than I remember.
Without the usual whooshing
and ticking of the machines,
the quiet drums
against my ears.

I take my grandmother's
old wool blanket
off my bed,
and cover Jonah's legs.

We don't go to church,
and I'm not sure I believe
in souls,
but I try to feel Jonah's soul
in the room.

What is it like
for the soul
to leave the body?
In the quiet of the room,
I feel a deep sadness
around me.

Is it Jonah's soul
saying a last goodbye
to his life on earth,
before moving on?

I hope,
when he gets to heaven,
or wherever he goes,
it's as big and beautiful and shining
as Blee-ah.

Wish

Dr. Kate arrives.
She doesn't say anything
about the cans on the lawn,
or Jonah's friends
standing outside.

She leans over and listens to Jonah
with her stethoscope.
I had no idea
that a doctor would listen
for what isn't there.

When she stands up,
she hangs her stethoscope
back around her neck.

I'm sorry, Liv,
Dr. Kate says.

I gave my birthday wish
to Jonah,
I tell her,
for him to have whatever he
wanted most.
Is this what he wanted?

I don't know,
she answers.

What made him get so sick
so fast?
I ask her.
I thought he would get better.
That we were doing
all we could.

It was pneumonia, Liv,
and he was too weak
to fight it.
It wasn't anyone's fault.

I blame Jonah for three things.
One
Not thinking about me
when he picked up the gun.
Two
Always looking so far ahead
into his future,
that he missed seeing
all the good things
right in front of him.
Three
Leaving me alone
again.

At four thirty a.m.,
after Elinor comes

after Johnny hugs me goodbye,
after Mom lets
Jonah's body
be taken away,
I find the number
for the Brann farm.

When a man answers,
I say,

Sorry to wake you up,
but I need to get a message
to Clay LeBlanc.

You didn't wake me.
I've already had my breakfast
and two cups of coffee.

I recognize the voice
of the very old man.

Could you wake Clay
and ask him to pick me up
at home?

Your young man shouldn't need waking,
he says,
he should be out in the barn.
I'm headed there now.
I'll let him know.

Because he is nice enough
not to ask why—
why I called so early
why I need Clay to come get me—
I tell him.

My brother died this morning.

There is silence on the phone,
and then he speaks:

My twin brother died when we were ten,
got his hand caught in the corn chopper.

I'm sorry,
I say,
and hang up,
because I'm crying for Jonah,
and crying for the little farm boy
who didn't get to grow up
to be a very old man
with his brother.

Moms

By the time Clay gets there
in his red truck,
the sun has come all the way up.

I'll be back later,
I call out to Mom and Elinor
as I head out the door.

Clay is standing on the sidewalk
in front of our house.
When I reach him,
his arms go around me,
and my arms wrap around him.
Over his shoulder,
I see Gwen
in the window of Number 24.

Mom alert, I say,
Gwen's watching us.

Same over here,
he says,
and when I turn my head
Mom is there
in the front window
of Number 23.

I wave to Mom,
then wave to Gwen,
get into the red truck,
and pull the door closed.
When the truck pulls out,
all that is left for the moms
to see
is each other.

Sorry it took me so long.
I had to help finish the milking.
Mr. Brann told me
about Jonah.

I put my hand out the window
and try to feel Jonah's soul
in the wind.
How fast do souls travel?
Do they start out slow,
then pick up speed
when they get near the end
of their journey?

I have something to show you
at the farm,
Clay says,
something Mr. Brann thinks you'd like to see.

I Meet an Organic Baby Cow

The "something" is a baby organic cow,
lying on straw in a pen in the barn.
Its head and body are splotched black and white,
its ears are black and its nose is pink.

It's so cute!
I gush.
And it's true.
Its legs are tucked
underneath itself,
and it watches me with its
big dark eyes.

The very old man looks at the baby cow
like it never occurred to him
that it could be
cute.

She's a week old tomorrow,
weighs just about seventy pounds,
and drinks two quarts of milk
twice a day.

I can't help it—
the laughter makes its way
out of my mouth.
Mr. Brann has just played

Three Things with us,
and he doesn't even know it.

Clay is smiling
and holds up three fingers.

The very old farmer
seems pleased with himself
that he's made me happy
with his facts about the calf.

And for a second,
I feel Jonah in the barn with us,
flashing past,
like a bright comet heading out of the
solar system.

Does she have a name?
I ask the farmer.

A name?
He repeats my question.
Not that I know of.

The corners of his mouth turn up
just a little,
and I realize he's making a joke,
and I laugh again.

Trailer

Clay takes me to see
where he is living.
The boys at school
are right,
that it's a trailer
behind the barn.
I've never been in
such a very old trailer.
It's rounded at the ends
where the wall and ceiling meet,
and everything in the kitchen
is miniature—
a tiny sink next to a tiny stove—
and the windows are so high
I can't see out of them
unless I jump.

There's a little wooden table
with two chairs,
almost big enough for two people
to eat at.

Half the table is covered with books.
I read the titles:
Organic Dairy Production

Grass-Fed Cattle
Essential Guide to Calving

It looks to me like Clay
is also doing his own
independent study project.

Where do you sleep?
I ask him.

Clay points to a long, brown-colored couch.
There's a bedroom down the hall,
but it doesn't heat very well,
so I sleep here.
It's pretty comfortable.

Clay opens a tiny refrigerator.
Would you like something to drink?
I have milk and orange juice.

Is the milk from the organic cows?

Yes, it is.

Then I'll have some.

Clay pours milk from a big glass jar
into a mug and hands it to me.

The milk is thick and creamy,
and it doesn't taste like any milk
I've had before.
I drink it slowly and
watch Clay walk around
the dollhouse trailer.
He looks different.
His face and the back of his neck
are sunburned.
He is looking more like a farmer
than a bug killer.

Clay comes and sits on the couch
next to me,
and takes my hand.
He brings it to his mouth
and kisses it.
I lean against him.

Do you want to talk about Jonah?
he asks me.

No, not now,
I say.

So we don't.

PART FIVE

Moo

I want to say goodbye
to the baby organic cow
before Clay takes me back,
so we stop to see her
in the barn.

This time she's standing up
and comes over to the fence—
close enough that I can pet
the white part of her forehead
between her ears.
Her baby cow skin
feels both tough and soft.

Then she goes over to the corner
of the pen and drinks water
from a black rubber bucket.
I don't ask Clay why
she isn't with her mother,
or why her mother
isn't with her.
I don't really want to know.
I just like watching
water drip from her mouth
when she lifts her face up
from the bucket.
I look back at her
with my human eyes

that are next to each other
rather than on either side
of my head.

MOOOOO. MOOOOOOO,
she cries.
It's true, I learn—
cows, even baby organic cows,
really do say moo.

I don't ask him to,
but Clay drives very slowly
along the turns of the river,
back to DEAD END.

Look in the glove compartment,
he says.

I open the glove compartment,
and there's a cell phone.
Is that yours?
I ask.

Yes, I forgot your number,
so enter it if you want.
And put mine in your phone.

Why now?
I ask him.

I guess it was time,
he says.

I think of joking with him,
saying "welcome to the
twenty-first century"
or "do you still know
how to use one?"
but I don't.
Instead, I put my name
in his contacts,
all in capitals
LIV
like the letters on my canoe.

When we pull up in front of
Number 23,
there are no cans
on the lawn,
and all the medical equipment
is gone.

The strange thing
about Number 24
is that nothing has changed
since we left—
the Bugz Away van hasn't moved
from the spot it was in,
Gwen's car is in the same place,
and the lights are still on

in the house.
Clay's parents have to have seen
the black hearse
that came for Jonah,
and maybe they're afraid of what Mom
will throw
if they step outside.

I can see Clay, like Gwen,
trying to decide
where the line is,
and what side
he's on.

I can come in with you,
Clay offers.

I think about Mom screaming,
and Gwen
watching Jonah's body
wheeled out of the house.

*You should probably check
on your mother,*
I say.
*Call me later.
You have the number now
in your phone.*

For Sale

Just like I wanted
when I first made the deal
with Gwen,
a week after Jonah dies,
a moving van pulls up
to Number 24,
and loads beds, dressers,
boxes, chairs, and even,
I suppose,
the gun safe.

I don't see Gwen
before they leave.
I don't get
one more hug.
I check the mailbox,
and it's empty.
I was hoping there might be
a last square
of fudge.
For the first time,
I wish I had something
to give Gwen,
but she is gone.

A week after that,
a FOR SALE sign
is on their lawn.

Clay tells me his parents
moved to Land O' Lakes, Florida.
There is actually a town
with that name.

Why Florida?
I ask Clay.
*Are there more bugz there
than in Maine?*

Actually,
Clay says,
*I don't know if there's more,
but a lot of them are bigger.
For instance,
there are huge mosquitoes there
called gallinippers,
twenty times larger
than most mosquitoes.
Also, Florida has the palmetto bug,
a large species of cockroach
that is about an inch and a half long.*

Clay holds up his thumb and forefinger
to show me how big that is.

Since Jonah died,
we stopped playing the
Three Things game—
maybe because that was something

we did with Jonah—
so I don't ask Clay
if he knows the name
of a third giant bug
that lives in Florida.

It's just me and Mom now
in Number 23.
Jonah's hospital bed is gone
from the living room,
the schedule is gone from the
refrigerator,
but we still spend
most of our time
in the kitchen.

Mom asks me if I mind
if she stays in my old room upstairs.
I could have her and Dad's big room
facing the street.
I tell her I like my
little cubbyhole of a room
downstairs.

I leave a light on
in the kitchen
at night,
and a fan whirring
in my room.
I guess I got used to
falling asleep to the sound of O,

and the nurses doing their quiet work
at the sink.

I miss them all,
especially Johnny, Vivian, and Phoebe.
They weren't only on Jonah's side,
they were on my side, too.

At the Great Water Place

You know,
Mom says to me one evening
a few weeks later
while we eat pizza she picked up
after work,
your counselor says you turned in a very impressive—
those were his words—independent project report.
So you will be able to continue on
to your junior year.

Oooh, lucky me!
I make a little circle in the air
with one finger.

Sometime, maybe you could show it to me,
your report.
He said it was about the Kennebec River,
and the old mills around here.

Sure, if you want to see it,
I say.

How does it start?
Mom asks me.

You mean, the beginning?
I ask her.

Yes, the beginning.

If you really want to know,
it starts:
"The name 'Kennebec'
comes from the Abenaki
and one translation means
'at the great water place.'"

Very nice. I'd like to read it.

Also,
Mom is on a roll,
I'm aware that you go out on the river.
I can see the canoe from upstairs.
It's good that you wear a life jacket.

You're telling me this because . . . ?
I ask her.
The pizza has mushrooms and olives,
and I start in on my second piece.

And, she says,
not answering my question,
whenever you want,
you should invite Clay
into the house.
He doesn't always have to wait for you
outside, in his truck.

When Mom says that,
I realize
I thought I was protecting Mom
from having Clay
in the house,
but it's me
who's not ready—yet—
to have Clay see
what it's like now.

How empty the house feels
without Jonah.

Okay, I get it,
I say,
and thanks for getting
my favorite toppings.

Tornado

Sweet Sunflower/Audrey
is back from the hospital,
all recovered from her asthma attack,
and Hunter invites me over.

I can't,
I say to Hunter.
Maybe another time.

I have no reason
to say no,
and I don't
give him an excuse.

I still wear the
stone of the heart
Sara and Rainie gave me,
and I'm glad his sister is better,
that she came home
to run around with all her
brothers and sisters.
Even, one day,
with the new one.
Sara is pregnant,
Rainie told me,
and Hunter will have a new hippie sib
in the fall.

Our family is cut in half,
and Hunter's family is growing.
I've read about tornadoes
that hit one house
with such force
that it's flattened,
while the house next to it
comes through the storm
unscathed.

I'm afraid if I went
to Hunter's house,
I'd say what no one
wants to hear.

You are lucky
the bad thing
didn't happen to you.
It doesn't make you
better than everyone else.
And it doesn't mean
it won't get you
next time.

Yes, for now,
it's better
for everyone
if I stay
away.

Then I hear the quiet
on Hunter's end of the phone,
him wondering if he said something wrong,
why I'm pushing him away,
if I'm mad because his sister is fine
and my brother is not.

When you get a chance, though, Hunter,
I could use some help,
I say.

Sure, anything.

I can hear how relieved he is.

I found envelopes with seeds
my father saved,
tomato and cucumber seeds,
from the garden
he kept in the backyard.
Only tomatoes and cucumbers,
that's what he grew every year.
I want to grow them myself,
but I don't know what to do.

You should start the tomatoes
indoors,
Hunter says.

Yes, that's what Dad did.
In all these containers
by the window.

I'll come over
and help you get them started.
It'll be fun,
Hunter says.

Thanks, Hunter,
and if they grow,
I'll invite you over this summer for
tomato and cucumber sandwiches,
you and all your
brothers and sisters.

Once the tornado passes,
one neighbor
picks up the pieces,
looks for what's left
of their possessions
under the rubble,
finding room
in their heart
to accept their neighbor's help.

Verdict

I don't know why it is,
that you can wait and wait
your hardest for something,
and it always comes
when you've finally
given up hope.

What do we all think
the verdict will do?
Turn back time?
Make right what went wrong
in the attic?
Punish Clay's father?
All of those things?

The verdict is mailed
to Birchell,
who comes to the house
with it.

He reads the judge's words out loud:

"A revolver is a lethal weapon
whose sole function is to kill human beings
and animals of comparative size.
A person owning a weapon of this kind
has a duty to exercise reasonable care

under the circumstances,
to see no harm would be visited upon
others as a consequence of his conduct.
A majority of other jurisdictions have
considered it actionable negligent entrustment
for a person to leave a firearm in a place
where he should foresee it might fall
into the hands of a minor.
Under the circumstances, reasonable care
requires the owner of a firearm either
to keep ammunition in a separate location
or, if the firearm is loaded, to keep it secured
in a place where minors cannot access
the firearm.
In this case the evidence demonstrates
that the defendant's conduct in leaving
a loaded weapon on a windowsill
created a reasonably foreseeable
catastrophic injury."

Basically,
Birchell says,
*the judge is saying that the owner of the gun
has a responsibility to keep it out of the hands
of minors.*

I get that,
Mom says.

He continues reading:

"Comparative negligence allows the plaintiff
to recover from the defendant even if partially
at fault, but only for the percentage
the defendant was at fault.
Maine is a modified comparative fault
jurisdiction, meaning that the plaintiff
can recover damages only if he is less than
fifty percent responsible for his own injuries.
I will consider the actions of Jonah Carrier
in picking up the firearm and pulling the trigger
negligent and a substantial factor
in causing his own injuries at twenty-five percent,
and the actions of the defendant Arthur LeBlanc,
in negligent entrustment of a firearm,
in not safely storing the firearm,
and leaving a loaded gun accessible to a minor,
negligent at seventy-five percent."

What does that mean?
Mom asks.

I answer before Birchell has a chance.

*She's saying Jonah was twenty-five percent responsible,
and Mr. LeBlanc was seventy-five percent responsible
for what happened.*

Mom gets up from her chair
and paces around the kitchen.

The judge is saying my son
is responsible for what happened
to him?

Mrs. Carrier,
Birchell says,
what matters here is that the judge thinks
Mr. LeBlanc is more than fifty percent
responsible. She is agreeing with us.
You won the claim.

Jonah is twenty-five percent responsible?
Mom asks Birchell again.

Mom,
I say,
it's just a number.
The judge is saying you won
the lawsuit.
Right?
I ask Birchell.

Yes. Birchell turns the page.
And she is awarding you $600,000
for our claim of negligent entrustment of a firearm.

I can do the math in my head.
And you get $200,000 of that,
I say to Birchell.

There is also an award for
wrongful death, for loss of the child's
comfort, society, and companionship,
Birchell starts reading from the page
when Mom interrupts.

Wrong death?

WrongFUL death,
Birchell repeats.
Remember after Jonah passed,
I said that I would amend the complaint
from action for loss of services
to wrongful death.

Mom sits back down.

The judge has awarded you $300,000
for wrongful death,
$200,000 for conscious pain and suffering,
and $1,500 for funeral expenses.

Whose pain and suffering?
Mom asks.

Birchell looks embarrassed by the question.

That would be Jonah's.

How did the judge figure out a number
for what Jonah felt
in the belly of the whale?

I do the math again.
$300,000 total for wrongful death.
Birchell gets one-third, or $100,000, of that.
He gets one-third of the money
for Jonah's conscious pain
and suffering.
And probably one-third
of the award for funeral expenses.

Still, that gives Mom
over $700,000.

Do Clay's parents
have that much money?
I ask Birchell.
I think
of Gwen's worn bathrobe
and scuffed slippers.

The award will be paid by their homeowner's
policy. It was their insurance company that hired the
lawyer for them.

Birchell hands Mom the papers
from the judge
to read for herself.

I thought the lawsuit
was all about the money,
but now I'm not sure.

This is what I learn, too.
Even when you wait and hope
for the thing you think
will solve everything,
it doesn't always happen
the way
you imagine.

PART SIX

Driver's Ed

After the verdict,
the check comes.
Mom doesn't buy a new car
or take us on a trip,
but she does have the roof leak fixed.

I like the simulator machine
at the driver's ed class,
but the first time I sit
in the driver's seat
of the real car,
I look down at my hands
on the steering wheel
and freeze.

I don't think this is a good idea,
I tell the driving instructor.
I have a better idea.
Why don't YOU sit in the driver's seat,
and if I see YOU doing something wrong,
I'll use that special brake
on the passenger side—
to stop you,
so you'll know I know
what to do.

The driving instructor
is speechless for a minute,
then shouts at me.

I thought I'd heard everything
from you kids.
Liv, there's nothing humorous
about learning to drive.
If you're not ready,
do me a favor and get out of the car.
And don't come back until you're prepared
to follow the rules.

I get out of the car.

Plant Obsessed

I decide there are better things
to do in the summer
than driver's ed.

Like growing tomatoes and cucumbers
in my father's garden.

My hands have a permanent stain of dirt
on them,
and my arms and legs are full of black fly
and mosquito bites.
I know I am giving the seedlings way more attention
than they need—
that Rainie and Justine think
I'm plant obsessed—
but when they taste their first
tomato and cukes and mayo and salt sandwich,
they'll understand.

*Uh-oh, Liv, I think I see a green baby worm
under a tomato leaf on that plant,*
Justine says.

She is sunning herself on a chaise longue
in the backyard.

Rainie points to the little wooden platforms
I put under the cucumbers,
so they don't sit directly on the soil.

*Do they really need their own little beds
to sleep on?*

Yes, they do. They really do,
I answer.

That makes Justine and Rainie and even Piper laugh.

Piper surprises me
by becoming a little plant obsessed too.
She likes to water the tomatoes
with the garden hose,
adjusting the nozzle
so it sprays down
like a gentle rain,
watching how water-washed leaves
look a little greener.

Summer

I swim off the dock
by the eddy
every day,
even in the rain.

Clay's day off
we swim
in our shorts and T-shirts.

I go underwater,
my hair floating above me.
When I come up
I hear Clay.

I love you, Liv.
I have for a while.

A while? What's a while?

Ever since I watched what you did
to your father's cement pad
three summers ago.

It's just like Clay
to give me a thought-out
explanation,
with a time
and a place.

I didn't know anyone saw me,
I say.

Dad had poured cement
for a new patio area
in front of the house,
to replace the cracked and broken
slab Mom hated.

The cement needs
twenty-four hours
to dry,
Dad said,
so don't walk on it
until tomorrow.

When Dad went inside,
I didn't walk on it.

I put my hair in a knot
on top of my head,
leaned way over the
wooden sawhorses
Dad had left as barriers,
and hand-printed my way
across the wet cement.

I was so busy
making my patio design,
I had no idea Clay was watching
from across the street.

Yes, Clay said,
it was my father who pointed out
what you were doing.
He said, There's the girl for you, Clay,
a beautiful rule bender,
that's what you need.
Help you lighten up a bit.

The half of my body
out of the water
feels like it's frying
in the sun.

I don't have explanations
for Clay,
when and how it happened—
it just did.

I press my river-water lips
to his lips,
and dive back under the water,
taking his words with me
when I go.

Ashes

Dad's ashes
and Jonah's ashes
are side by side
in their cardboard boxes
on a shelf
in Mom's closet.

I shut myself in the closet,
to see how it feels.
The slats on the louvered doors
only let in a little light
so it's always dim
even in the middle
of the day.

I know where Jonah's ashes
need to go.

I take the box
from the closet
and carry it downstairs.

Mom is out on the front lawn,
smoking.
She started again
after the verdict.
So much money,

she told me,
it's a lot of responsibility.

It's not like she got a new puppy,
it's $700,000,
money enough to fix
all the roof leaks
for the rest of her life.

But I don't walk in Mom's shoes.

Mom says there's money for school now,
even enough for an out-of-state college,
but I'm not sure
and I don't want to go
out of state.
The thing is—
it will never feel right
to spend Jonah's money
on me.

I did think of some things
to do—
show people who feel broken
by what they've lost
how the river thunders
when the ice
goes out,
the way cows stand
so still

in a green field,
and how Hunter's fiddle music
reminds you
what it feels like
to love this world.

I could even learn
to make fudge.

Mom and I both look out at Number 24.
The FOR SALE sign
is leaning to one side,
and the grass is getting long.
The pear tree on their front lawn
has tiny fruits.

She sees what I'm holding
in my hands.

I'm taking the canoe
out on the river.
Is that okay?
I ask her.

We both know
I never ask
to use my canoe—
that I'm really asking
something else.

Mom blows the smoke
to her side,
away from me,
and nods her head yes.

You can come, too,
I say,
if you want.

Okay, I'll be right there,
Mom answers,
like she was just waiting
for me to ask her.

River

When she comes out
the back door,
Mom has Dad's box
in her hands.

When we paddle off
from the shore,
Dad's box is on Mom's lap,
and Jonah's box rocks
in the bottom of the canoe.

It's one of those
half-cloudy, half-sunny days,
when the river is dark
in some places,
and lit up in other places.

It's that time of year
when the river comes alive—
white water lilies,
purple arrowhead plants,
and a row of mallard ducks.

It feels like we are having
a family moment,
all together
in one place.

I paddle us
to the whirlpools
at the bend
in the river—
the place where you can't tell
if the water
will take you upstream or downstream
or round and round
in a beautiful circle.

I take Jonah's box
from the bottom
of the canoe,
open the top,
and tip it out
over the whirlpools.

Jonah's ashes
arc into the water.

Mom gives Dad's ashes
to the river, too.

I already felt
Jonah's soul,
if that's what it was,
saying goodbye to me
in the barn
with the baby organic cow,

but now
whatever else is left
is also free.

Most of Jonah's ashes
disappear into the whirlpools
of turning water,
but not all.

Clay would have
a physics equation
to explain
why the force of the wind
and the angle I held Jonah's box
blew some ashes
back onto my hands.

Should we say something?
Mom asks me.

I don't know,
I answer,
it's up to you.

Goodbye,
Mom says,
*I don't think there's anything wrong
with saying goodbye.*

I press my stone-of-the-heart necklace
hard against my chest.

The clouds move
and the sun suddenly
lights up the whole eddy.
I reach over
the side of the canoe,
and my ashy hands
make their own swirls
in the river,
round and round,
round and round,
until even I can't tell
what direction
they're going.

Acknowledgments

Thank you to my wonderful agent, Steven Chudney, who gave me a chance and has been the best guide I could hope for throughout this journey. You are there every step of the way with your kindness, humor, and knowledge.

I couldn't be more thrilled that this novel found its perfect home with editor Tara Weikum. Your editorial vision, skill, and understanding made it the book it was meant to be.

With appreciation to the whole team at HarperCollins, including Sarah Homer, Renée Cafiero, Allison Brown, Ebony LaDelle, and Michael D'Angelo, and to Chris Kwon and Alison Donalty for the gorgeous cover and book design.

Jennifer Reed, who shone a light so I could see where I needed to go. And held my hand along the way.

Thank you to writers Cathy McKelway, Sally Stanton, and Melanie Ellsworth for being the best critique partners and for laughter, lunches, and encouragement.

I am indebted to my early readers, Vickie Limberger, AnnMarie Limberger, Sylvane Pontin, and David Axelman, and early encouragers, Yolanda Kolinski, Eric Boulton-Bailey, and Eileen and Bill Culley. Special thanks to Ann Dorney, for her medical knowledge, Peter Bickerman, for his legal expertise, and H. D. Ammerman, for insight into the pulp and paper industry in Maine.

To Rachel and Bradley, for all your support.

To my husband, Denis, for this beautiful life and for listening to the words.

And always, my love to the children and families who welcomed me as a nurse into their homes and their lives. It was a privilege to be there.